The Advent of Stickleback Hollow

The Mysteries of Stickleback Hollow

By C.S. Woolley

A Mightier Than the Sword UK Publication

©2020

The Advent of Stickleback Hollow

The Mysteries of Stickleback Hollow

By C. S. Woolley

A Mightier Than the Sword UK Publication

Paperback Edition

Paperback ISBN 978-0-9951472-0-1

Hardback ISBN 978-0-9951472-1-8

ePub ISBN ISBN 978-0-9951472-2-5

Kindle ISBN 978-0-9951472-3-2

iBook ISBN 978-0-9951472-4-9

For Lesley

The best mother-in-law I could ask for

Author's Note

Thanks for taking the time to read *The Advent of Stickleback Hollow*, its been a long time coming, and my apologies for the delay - moving to a new country slows down the creative process somewhat.

It is the run-up to Christmas, and though there is little for the characters to be joyful about at this moment in time, Stickleback Hollow is still alive with the Christmas Spirit. This is one of the few books in the series, like *the March of the Berry Pickers,* that contains a mystery that is not part of the wider narrative of the series. It is a simple story of how even when we face the most trying of times, there is some hope to be found.

The Characters

Lady Sarah Montgomery Baird Watson-Wentworth

The heroine

Bosworth

The butler

Mrs Bosworth

The housekeeper

Cooky

The cook

Mr Alexander Hunter

A huntsman and groundskeeper of Grangeback

Pattinson

An Akita, Alexander's hunting dog

Constable Arwyn Evans

Policeman in Stickleback Hollow

Doctor Jack Hales

The doctor in Stickleback Hollow

Stanley Baker

Son of Miss Baker

Lee Baker

Son of Miss Baker

Reverend Percy Butterfield

The vicar in Stickleback Hollow

Mr Thomas Egerton

Son of Wilbraham & Elizabeth

Mrs Charlotte Egerton nee Milner

Wife of Thomas

Mr Edward Christopher Egerton

Son of Wilbraham & Elizabeth

Miss Mary Pierrepont

Fiancée of Edward

Edryd Evans

A welsh gentleman, farmer and father of Arwyn and Derwyn

Derwyn Evans

A welsh gentleman, brother of Arwyn, son of Edryd

Mr Mitchell Claydon

An explorer

Miss DeVill

A young lady of Stickleback Hollow

Miss Beaumont

A retired governess

Chapter 1

A man's sorrow is never so great as when he has lost all hope. November had drifted by in something of a haze. There had been the bonfire to celebrate the 5th November, but beyond that, there had been nothing close to celebrations in Stickleback Hollow.

Lady Sarah Montgomery Baird Watson-Wentworth was in hospital. She had been since the Berry Pickers festival had been marred by the appearance of a witch.

Some rumours in the village said that she had been cursed by the witch when she was taken, whilst others blamed the cold weather for striking down the young lady. Neither of these was true. The stress of the supernatural events that had surrounded the Berry Pickers Festival had caused her ladyship to miscarry.

She had been secretly pregnant with the child of Mr Alexander Hunter. Mr Hunter was the groundskeeper at Grangeback Manor, the estate which the village of Stickleback Hollow belonged to.

But he was not simply a functionary that had seduced the lady of the house. He was the illegitimate son of Brigadier George Webb-Kneelingroach, the Lord of Grangeback, and Mr Hunter was deeply in love with the young lady.

Lady Sarah was the ward of the brigadier and had been since she had arrived from India following the death of both her parents. Though she had family in London, she much preferred the company of her father's former commanding officer and the society of the North to that of the South.

The brigadier had known of the relationship developing between the pair, and when it was clear that they meant to marry, he put aside his pride in order to recognise Mr Hunter as his son and heir.

But before the brigadier could legally recognise his son, he had been called away on a clandestine affair. No one had heard from George Webb-Kneelingroach and knew very little of where he was. It was not even certain if he would ever be able to return home.

In his absence, Doctor Hales, the brigadier's oldest friend, had moved in to Grangeback Manor to help Lady Sarah oversee the daily running of the great estate and advise her on affairs in the village.

Mr Hunter and her ladyship had still been able to steal time alone together, especially in the darkest hours of the night. Something which had led to Lady Sarah's pregnancy.

She had been overjoyed to learn she was pregnant, and though he feared for Lady Sarah's reputation, Mr Hunter had been thrilled as well.

But that delight was now but a distant memory, as faded as paper left out in the sun. Mr Hunter had not seen Lady Sarah since she had been admitted to the hospital. It was not because he did not care that he did not visit the woman he loved.

There were many complicated reasons that Mr Hunter held as good enough to wait for her to return to Stickleback rather than sit at her bedside.

The first of these reasons was that he was simply a groundskeeper and hunter. He had no social standing and as far as society was concerned, he was the help and it would be inappropriate for him to sit beside the sick lady of the manor. He had not been legally recognised as the brigadier's son, and until he was, he was nothing more than a pauper.

The second reason was he did not want anyone to know that he was the father of the baby that Lady Sarah had lost. Such a revelation would cause a scandal that her reputation would never recover from. He had known since their romance had begun that there was a risk Lady Sarah would be publicly shamed and shunned if their love affair was discovered, and though he did not want to ruin her, he could not stay away from her when she was only a few lawns away.

His third reason was that someone had to stay behind to take care of Grangeback. With the doctor at the hospital so often and guests in the house, he was needed where he was.

The fourth and final reason was that he did not want to look at Lady Sarah and discover that she now hated him. He had impregnated her, he had not saved her in time from the witch during the festival, and her life had been put in danger because of his actions. He often lay awake at night wondering what possible reasons she could have to love him now after she had endured all of that because of him.

None of his thoughts or reasons for remaining at Grangeback had been spoken aloud, and only the doctor had dared to even attempt to talk to Mr Hunter about accompanying him to the hospital.

Alex had declined and locked himself in George's study for the rest of the day. Pattinson, his Akita, had spent a few hours scratching at the door. That is until Mrs Bosworth had scolded the dog and taken him to the kitchen where Cooky could spoil him.

It was not only Mr Hunter that had sunk into a melancholy state. Cooky, the cook, was normally a very bright and bustling woman, but since Lady Sarah had been taken to the hospital, she had barely smiled or fussed over anything. Mrs Bosworth had spied Cooky hugging Pattinson on more than one occasion as she wept into his long fur.

The housekeeper had not mentioned this to anyone and had left Cooky to deal with her worries in her own way. Mrs Bosworth had her own burden of guilt that she bore. She had known about the relationship between Lady Sarah and Mr Hunter. She had even known about their multiple midnight rendezvous. Yet, she had done nothing to stop them.

The housekeeper blamed herself for the current state of the atmosphere in Grangeback and Lady Sarah's hospital admittance. Her husband, Bosworth, the butler, had tried to persuade his wife that none of it was her doing, but to no avail.

Edryd and Derwyn Philips were the only people at Grangeback to not feel some form of responsibility for Lady Sarah's misfortune. Edryd was the father of Derwyn and Arwyn, the local policeman down in Stickleback Hollow. Edryd and Derwyn had come to visit Arwyn a few months before in an attempt to repair the family rift that had existed between them for many years.

They had been invited to stay at the manor, and they had enjoyed the hospitality, as well as the chance to spend so much time with Arwyn, but now Edryd felt out of place and was longing for home. He had thought of leaving weeks ago, but he had remained to keep an eye on Derwyn.

Derwyn was a headstrong man and one that had never had much luck with women. That was until he had met Miss DeVille, a woman who lived in Stickleback Hollow. Derwyn and Miss DeVille had been almost inseparable since they had met and Edryd was concerned that the pair were rushing into an ill-advised romance.

Yet, as the weeks had gone by, the pair had proven to be a good match, and any objection that Edryd might have had to the match were no more.

Arwyn had been to the hospital to visit Lady Sarah several times and had done his best to not speak of Mr Hunter to her. He could see the pain on the lady's face when he arrived without her lover, but she never said a word about what she was feeling.

"Someone needs to do something," Arwyn said to Doctor Hales as he left Lady Sarah's hospital room.

"It is none of our business," Doctor Hales warned the constable as he steered him down the corridor of the hospital.

"It is our business. They are both our friends. The brigadier approves of their match, and all they are doing is hurting themselves," Arwyn argued.

"There is something that you learn after you have seen as much of the world as I have," the doctor sighed, "When it comes to affairs of the heart, you can't stop people from doing stupid things."

"But surely they would listen to common sense," Arwyn argued.

"People in love often leave all thought and common sense behind - especially when they are in great pain. We cannot interfere. It is up to them to find a way to reconcile and repair the hurt they are both feeling. It is part of being in love. If they cannot, then they will not be able to weather the storms that life can throw against them," Doctor Hales replied.

The doctor had left the constable to think about what he had said and hoped that he would listen to the wisdom he'd shared. However, Jack Hales did not hold out much hope. Not for Mr Hunter and Lady Sarah, not for Constable Evans refraining from interfering, and not for a happy outcome to the whole situation.

Chapter 2

Mrs Bosworth did not sleep well. She had not had a good night's sleep since Lady Sarah had been taken to the hospital. Her mind was clouded with worry, and the lack of sleep combined with this worry made her extremely irritable.

Not a soul in Grangeback dared to speak to her for fear of irritating. She stomped about in a foul mood; one of barely contained rage and frustration. One poorly chosen word was all it would take to cause Mount Bosworth to erupt and cover everyone in her path in her rage. So silence hung heavily in the air of the manor house.

With Lady Sarah absent, there was also no one to play host to Edryd and Derwyn Evans. Derwyn spent almost no time in the house, and even if he did, it was unlikely that he would have noticed the change in the atmosphere in the house.

But for Edryd, it was difficult for him to find things to occupy his time. Originally the pair were not going to stay long in Stickleback Hollow, but with Derwyn and Miss

DeVille's relationship blossoming, and Edryd keen to repair his relationship with Arwyn, the pair decided to remain for a few months. Edryd had written to his wife and farm manager to inform them of their decision. He promised to let them know when to expect their return in a later letter.

His wife had been very understanding, and his farm manager had been keen for the opportunity to prove that he was more than equal to the task of looking after the family holdings without the guiding hands of Edryd and Derwyn.

Without the presence of Lady Sarah, the brigadier, and Doctor Hales, Edryd was feeling decidedly lonely. The atmosphere that had been created in the house made him feel more than a little uncomfortable.

Mr Hunter was no companion in his current state either. The groundskeeper was not the best of company when the other members of the household were there, but with him locking himself in the brigadier's study for hours on end, the only companion that Edryd had in the house was Pattinson, the dog.

After his visit to the hospital, Arwyn had become busy as there had been a possible sighting of Grace and Millie that had led him, and some of the other constables from

Chester, to depart for a few weeks. Constable Clewes had arrived in Stickleback Hollow to oversee the village in Arwyn's absence.

Unfortunately, the sightings had proven to be a wild goose chase, and when Arwyn returned home, he was rather despondent.

Edryd understood how much Arwyn wanted to find the two missing women and how his son thought that his failure to bring them home was letting down Lady Sarah more than anyone else.

Edryd knew that Arwyn was concerned for the safety of the two missing women as well, but his son was very loyal to his friends and coupled with the sense of duty he felt towards to the family that inhabited Grangeback, it was not surprising that he was so frustrated by his failure.

Arwyn had waited until he knew that Doctor Hales would be at Grangeback and not at the hospital before he went to report his failure to the doctor and his father. He knew better than to expect Mr Hunter to greet him or for his brother to be at the house.

"You are pushing yourself too hard," Mrs Bosworth scolded him in a harsher tone than she would have ordinarily used, as she led Constable Evans through the halls of Grangeback to the drawing room where Doctor Hales and Edryd were sat.

Arwyn knew better than to reply to Mrs Bosworth and chose to walk in silence. Mrs Bosworth didn't stay anything else, not even when she opening the door to the drawing room, and slammed it again behind the constable.

"I see that things here haven't improved," the constable said dryly as he sat down in one of the large armchairs in the drawing room.

The room had two large sofas, and four high-backed armchairs all positioned around an elegant table in the centre. The room hadn't always looked this way; it was one of the many subtle changes which Lady Sarah had made to Grangeback Manor since her arrival.

The sofas faced each other, running parallel to long sides of the table, the four armchairs angled inwards at the corners, forming an open-ended rectangle. The fireplace stood at on end of the rectangle, and at the other was a card table and one of the many tables in the house that were well stocked with spirits in crystal decanters and appropriate glasses beside each.

Under the sofas, chairs and table was a large rug that came from Persia; the deep reds and blues in the carpet in stark contrast to the cream fabric of the sofas, the white marble of the fireplace, and the green leather of the chairs.

"No, things are as they were when you left," Doctor Hales sighed and stood to pour Arwyn a drink.

"How did you get on with your investigation?" Edryd asked as his son collapsed into the green leather of the armchair closest to the fire.

The fires in Grangeback were all blazing, keeping the house warm for the servants and masters alike. It was rather extravagant, but the brigadier had never been able to stand a cold house after his years in the military in hotter climates. Even though he was absent still, Bosworth had ordered the fires to be lit as his master could return at any moment.

"I didn't," Arwyn sighed in defeat, "It's as though Millie and Grace have both vanished from the face of the earth."

"Not vanished, they are just very well hidden. You'll find them, it will just take a little time," Jack tried to cheer up the young constable.

"Without knowing who did the kidnapping, I don't

see how we'll ever find them," Arwyn huffed.

"Hired men are only loyal to their employers as long as they get paid. There will be someone somewhere who can help you find these men. You just have to keep going, son. It's just a shame I won't be here to see you succeed," Edryd replied.

"What do you mean? Are you alright?" Arwyn asked anxiously as he sat bolt upright in his chair and looked between the doctor and his father.

"Calm yourself, your father isn't ill," Jack Hales said as he handed Arwyn a glass of whisky.

"Then you've decided to go home?" the constable asked.

"Yes. I've been away a long time as it is. Your mother can manage well enough, and there are plenty of young men looking to prove themselves, but I feel like I am more of a hindrance than a help now," Edryd said with a shrug.

"No, father, you're no hindrance," Arwyn chided his father.

"It is kind of you to say so, my boy, but I am under Mrs Bosworth's feet, Lady Sarah's condition is not being improved by me waiting in the house all day. I can't help

Doctor Hales; I can't even help you look for the two missing women. Your brother doesn't need me here, so it is best if I go back to Wales," Edryd concluded.

"Then, Derwyn is staying?" Arwyn asked.

"Yes, I believe his romantic entanglements will keep him here for some time. That's another reason I need to go back - prepare your mother for when Derwyn announces his engagement to an English girl. She'll faint clear away at the thought now," Edryd chuckled.

"Miss DeVille is a good woman, she'll make a good wife for him," Doctor Hales said as he settled back into his chair.

"You know my mother of old, doctor. The English are fine in small doses, but as family members, they are not very desirable - at least as far as a girl from the valleys is concerned," Arwyn yawned and sipped from his glass.

"Stay here tonight, Arwyn. Your brother will be back soon, and we should drink to your father before he leaves," the doctor instructed.

"When are you leaving?" Arwyn asked.

"Tomorrow morning. I would be unnecessary for me to stay another day," Edryd replied.

"Then I will stay, thank you, doctor. And thank you, father. These last few months have been, well," Arwyn stammered.

"You're welcome, lad. I feel the same," Edryd smiled at his son, "Jack, I hope you'll keep an eye on both my boys when I'm gone; make sure they don't get into too much trouble on their own?"

"Of course, it would be my pleasure," the doctor replied.

"Thank you. I'll also keep my eyes and ears open for any news on your two missing girls. Wales is as good a place as any to hide away," Edryd said warmly.

"Well, I suppose I should tell Mrs Bosworth to prepare some rooms for you, Arwyn," Doctor Hales shook his head at the thought of Mrs Bosworth's response to the request as the door to the drawing room opened, and Derwyn entered the room.

Chapter 3

The lodge was a small place that seemed to be completely unfit for a man as tall as Mr Hunter, but it was the one place he has always called home, and after all that happened, it was the one place he could be alone with his thoughts.

There were no lamps lit in the lodge, only the light of a small fire, by which Mr Hunter sat on a stool, his shoulders hunched over and a mug clenched firmly between the fingers of both hands.

He had never been much of a drinker. A beer or two was all that he would normally drink, mostly because he couldn't stand the taste, but it was better than the spirits that a lot of the public houses served.

But it was not beer that filled his mug now; it was gin. The dram houses of Chester had seen a lot of the young hunter in recent days. He had visited several different shops as he did not want to face the judgement of the store clerks as he bought increasing amounts of cheap gin.

The floor around the stool and hearth was littered with empty bottles, and it had been several hours since the groundskeeper had been able to see straight.

He was a failure in his own mind. He had failed to protect Lady Sarah from the witch, he had failed to resist his own baser instincts and not only was Lady Sarah now in hospital because of it, her reputation was sure to suffer when society discovered that she had been carrying his child.

He had lost his child and the grief he felt over the life that he would never know, never see grow, never call out to, only served to compound his failure.

Mr Hunter could not bring himself to visit Lady Sarah in the hospital. He could not bear to look at her frail form in the stark and sterile hospital room; to see the grief he felt reflected in his own eyes.

So he sat in front of the fire and drank to deaden the pain he felt. It worked for a time; until he drank so much that he collapsed on the floor of the lodge. But when he woke up, his body was stiff, his head pounded and the grief and failure came flooded back to his mind and threatened to crush him.

He brooded silently and had no company to stir him from his deepening depression. Alex had left Pattinson at the manor with Cooky and had no intention of collecting the dog.

He poured himself the last of the gin into his mug and was just about to drink when hammering fists on the lodge door broke his silent sulking.

"Go away," he slurred, without shifting his eyes from the fire.

The visitor did not respond. Instead, Mr Hunter heard the sound of a key scraping in the lock. He tried to get up, but before he had managed to reach his feet, the door to the lodge was thrown open and into the room marched Mrs Bosworth and Cooky, with Pattinson bounding beside them.

"You selfish little brat," Mrs Bosworth snapped and clipped Alex around the ear. In the hunter's inebriated state, the blow was enough to knock him to the ground.

"What was that for?" Alex scowled as he rubbed his ear and tired, unsuccessfully, to pull himself up.

"What do you think?" Mrs Bosworth spat, her eyes wide with fury, and her nostrils flared.

"Why are you sitting alone in the dark, reeking of gin, when the woman you love is in hospital?" Cooky asked, sensing that Mrs Bosworth and Mr Hunter were about to start an argument that would only go round in circles. The two women waited, but Alex gave no answer. He simply sat on the floor, amongst the empty bottles, his head hung low so he wouldn't have to look either of them in the eye.

"Hiding like a coward," Mrs Bosworth sneered.

"Now, now, Mrs Bosworth," Cooky soothed, "He's had a terrible loss to deal with. It's only natural to want some time to collect your thoughts. But I think we all know that the time has passed now, and it is time for you to go see her ladyship," Cooky said as she moved to Mr Hunter's side and tried to help him to his feet.

"Leave off," Alex said gruffly as he pulled away from Cooky and crashed into some of the bottles as he fell sideways. The sound of glass shattering made Cooky cluck as she turned Alex over. He had a nasty cut on his face and one on his hand. But neither was enough to calm Mrs Bosworth's rage.

"So, you sit and drink all of the brigadier's whisky and brandy in his study. You hide away from everyone and think you're the only one to ever lose something. Your father didn't fall this far when his wife and daughter died. Mr Bosworth didn't fall this far when our boys were taken from us. Abandon Lady Sarah, crawl back inside the bottle. Pickle yourself in this dark hole you've chosen. You won't be welcomed at the manor by any of us," Mrs Bosworth ranted as she looked own her nose at the hunter.

Cooky didn't try to stop her speaking this time, she knew when she could tame her friend's anger and when it was best to let her be. Instead, she bustled to the kitchen and found some tweezers, a clean rag and rubbing alcohol.

"Turn up the lamps please, Mrs Bosworth," Cooky said as she came back to Mr Hunter's side. She knelt beside the groundskeeper, where there was no broken glass.

Mrs Bosworth did as she was asked, and an uncomfortable silence fell on the room. With the extra light, Cooky began to carefully pull out the thin slivers of glass from each of Alex's wounds.

When she was sure she had removed all the glass, she wet the rag with the rubbing alcohol and then gently wiped down Mr Hunter's wounds.

"You've never been alone, you know," Cooky said as she began to clean the cut on Alex's face.

"I've been alone since my mother died," Mr Hunter whined and flinched as Cooky pressed the rag a little too hard against the wound.

"Nonsense. You've always had us, always had the brigadier. You've always chosen to keep to yourself. We respected that, knew it couldn't have been easy for you, not belonging to one world or another. But you seemed to settle and find yourself a life you liked. You weren't popular with the people in the village, but that seemed to work for everyone. So again, we let you be. But this time, this time you've gone very wrong," Cooky said sternly.

"I have the right to live how I please, so long as I steer clear of Arwyn and the paragons of virtue under the command of Captain Jonnes Smith," Alex replied as he tried to pull his face away from Cooky.

"Now, none of that. That childish behaviour is what gave you these bloody things. You don't want to go getting any more. And you are a fine one to speak about rights," Cooky scolded him.

"What do you mean?" Mr Hunter asked.

"She means you had no right to go rutting with a lady of higher social class in the house of your employer. You aren't her husband. For all you knew, you were rutting with the ward of your master, the man who took you in when you lost everything and gave you a home and a future. You didn't know you were his son. You had no right to her bed or her love, but you took it anyway," Mrs Bosworth said with contempt.

"That's none of your business," Alex yelled and pushed Cooky away.

"Is that so? Well, then, thank you for your hospitality. Really, you are a credit to your father," Cooky said spitefully as she threw down the rag, got quickly to her feet and walked purposefully to the door without looking back.

"If you want to be alone in this world, you are going the right way about it. Lady Sarah will recover, just in case you were wondering how she is. She can still have children, and I am sure there are plenty of men out there who will make her far happier than a snivelling drunk will," Mrs Bosworth said coldly.

"How did you know where I was?" Alex asked suddenly, his mood changing quickly under the influence of the alcohol and Mrs Bosworth's scorn.

"Lee and Stanley Baker followed you. They've been worried about you. Told us all about the dram shops you've been visiting too. I'm only glad they are tucked up in bed and not here to see you like this. It's a horrible thing to live to see your role models fall," Mrs Bosworth replied, shaking her head sadly, "Goodnight, Mr Hunter. I don't expect I'll be seeing you again."

Chapter 4

Miss Beaumont was a kind soul and one that had been distressed when she learned that Lady Sarah was in the hospital. Though Miss Beaumont did not spend a lot of time mixing in the same society as her ladyship, the former governess held the ward of the brigadier in the highest regard. Miss Beaumont also felt that she owed Lady Sarah a great debt as she felt that the young lady was responsible for her current happiness.

Mr Mitchell Claydon was an explorer with an international reputation, and it was thanks to Lady Sarah that Miss Beaumont and Mr Claydon had been introduced and had fallen in love.

Mr Claydon owned the largest house in the village of Stickleback Hollow, and he preferred the quiet of the country to the madness of London.

He was an anti-social creature that did not like the society of most people, so much so that from the time he arrived in Stickleback Hollow until he met Lady Sarah only

Mr Hunter had the honour of calling Mr Claydon a friend.

Now Mr Claydon was in love with the charming Miss Beaumont and had a handful of friends that he could call on or entertain when he felt the need.

Miss Beaumont adored Mr Claydon and was happy to walk through the woods around Stickleback Hollow in silence, just as long as Mr Claydon was by her side.

The pair were a good match, and with Miss DeVille spending so much time with Derwyn Evans, it seemed that both aunt and niece had been blessed with happiness thanks to the Grangeback Estate.

When news of Lady Sarah's admittance into hospital had reached the ears of Miss Beaumont, she had immediately insisted that she and Mr Claydon visit her.

Mr Claydon did not like to interfere in the business of others. He knew that Mr Hunter had an interest in Lady Sarah that went beyond friendship, and knew that the pair had been seen spending a lot of time together. This, coupled with Mr Hunter locking himself away from the world and not walking the woods or the grounds of Grangeback led Mr Claydon to believe that whatever had put Lady Sarah in the hospital involved Mr Hunter.

That type of situation was one that Mr Claydon knew was best to steer clear of.

But Miss Beaumont had insisted and even declared,

"If you feel so strongly, then I shall go without you. I would never have thought you to be so ungallant to allow me to go alone, nor so ungrateful that you would decline to visit such a charming and caring woman when she is ill."

That was all it took to get Mr Claydon to begrudgingly agree to go.

Mr Claydon kept a horse and trap that allowed him to get to London when necessary. It did not take him long to put the horse in its traces and help Miss Beaumont aboard.

He was not the best driver the world had known, but he was able to follow a road well enough. It took a few hours for them to reach the hospital as Mr Claydon had made a few wrong turns. The routes to London he knew well, but for an explorer, he was not gifted with a good sense of direction.

It often meant he was able to discover things that others would miss because they were heading the right way. He often consoled himself with the knowledge that Christopher Columbus had been trying to reach India when he discovered America.

"The best explorers are the ones that think they are going one way, but are in fact going the wrong way. That's when they find the best things," he had always said when people had questioned his inability to navigate.

Miss Beaumont sat quietly in the trap as Mr Claydon drove. She was happy to let him find his way. If he got lost, she knew the area better than most and would be able to put him back on the right path, but he did not need her nagging him. Miss Beaumont was a great believer in keeping quiet until people were ready to ask for help.

Despite the wrong turns, Mr Claydon managed to find his own way to the hospital. He left the horse in the care of the stable hands and escorted Miss Beaumont into the hospital.

It was a forbidding looking building from the outside, one that always looked grey and intimidating, even in sunshine. Inside, the halls smelt of sickness and urine, and the clacking of the heels of the nurses' shoes echoed down every corridor.

"Hello, can I help you?" a nurse looked up from her notes as the two entered. She offered them a warm smile, which Miss Beaumont returned.

"Yes, please. We are here to visit Lady Montgomery Baird Watson-Wentworth," Miss Beaumont replied.

"I'm sorry, but only visitors approved by Doctor Hales are allowed to visit her ladyship," the nurse said with slight condescension, though her smile stayed the same.

"How do you know we have not been approved by Jack?" Mr Claydon demanded in a gruff manner. The use of the doctor's first name seemed to shake the nurse slightly, but the brief crack in her composure was soon pasted over with the placid smile.

"I have a list," the nurse replied.

"And how would you know if we are on the list or not?" Miss Beaumont frowned, her patience wearing thin. She had dealt with the children of many rich and powerful individuals. Her patience had been tested many times, but she had learnt how to deal with difficult children, and as far as she was concerned, the nurse was nothing more than a difficult child.

"Because your names are not on the list," the nurse replied with a small smirk on her face.

"Ah so you know are names. Well, what talented staff they have here, my dear. They can read minds and know names of people the moment they lay eyes on their faces," Mr Claydon did not bother to veil his sarcasm. His voice was raised and echoed down the corridors. Some of the nurses and doctors walking the halls even paused to see what was happening at the front desk.

The nurse did not know how to reply, nor was she given the opportunity to as Doctor Hales hurried down the corridor.

"You're here, at last, I thought you were going to be here an hour ago!" Jack Hales grinned at Miss Beaumont and Mr Claydon as he held out his hand in greeting.

"Doctor, these people -" the nurse began, but the doctor held up his hand to quiet her.

"Mitchell drove," Miss Beaumont said with a wry smile, and the doctor laughed.

"Well, that certainly explains the delay. Did you give your names yet?" the doctor asked as he looked at the nurse, who blushed a deep crimson colour.

"Oh, we had no need. This woman is gifted with great powers of mind reading. She knew the moment we entered what our names were and that we weren't on the list," Mr Claydon bristled.

"Why did you not ask for their names?" Jack asked with a furrowed brow as he turned to the nurse.

"The way they are dressed, they are not the kind of visitors that her ladyship would be expecting," the nurse said defiantly.

"What a stupid girl you are," Miss Beaumont snapped, taking back both the doctor and Mr Claydon. They knew the placid side of her personality, neither had ever seen her as a strict governess disciplining wayward children.

"Excuse me?" the nurse bridled.

"You decided that based on our appearance we are unworthy of an association with Lady Sarah. Do you make such judgements about everyone that walks through these doors? Do you know who this man is? He is a renown explorer that has had private meetings with the king. He has been to more places than you can ever imagine and discovered more about this world than you shall ever know. I have spent my life educating the children of the most powerful people this country has known, and I have never dealt with someone so small-minded before in my life. Elizabeth Fry and I are well acquainted, and I am certain she will be very disappointed to learn of how terribly a nurse has behaved. Have you been to her school?" Miss Beaumont unleashed a tirade at the nurse but did not give her a chance to reply.

"I would suggest that in future when you are given a list that you ask for names before making such assumptions. Good day," Miss Beaumont swept away from the nurse, down the corridor in the direction that the doctor had come from. Doctor Hales and Mr Claydon exchanged impressed glances and hurried to catch her before Miss Beaumont became lost in the labyrinth of corridors.

"My dear, I have never been more proud to walk beside you," Mr Claydon smiled at Miss Beaumont as he took her arm.

"The world would be a much better place without the snap judgements of those who know so little but feel they know best," Miss Beaumont snorted as she tried to calm down.

"Come, she is this way," Doctor Hales said and beckoned for the pair to follow him.

The three walked in silence until they reached the room that Lady Sarah was recovering in. As the door swung open, the three could see Lady Sarah was sat up in the bed, reading *The Pickwick Papers.*

"Miss Beaumont, Mr Claydon, how wonderful to see you," her ladyship beamed as she placed a piece of cloth in the book and closed it.

"Oh! Lady Sarah! We were so worried, what a relief to see you looking so well. And I must say that is a most excellent choice of reading," Miss Beaumont fawned as she moved over to sit beside Lady Sarah.

"I am glad that I look so well. I am still very weak, and it will be sometime before I will be able to leave here and return home," Lady Sarah sighed.

"Well, at least we shall have some peace from all of your adventures whilst you are confined to your bed," Mr Claydon joked, and Lady Sarah chuckled.

"Quite. Oh, I do hope you can stay awhile and tell me of everything that has happened in the village. No detail is too small, not even a story about the Reverend Butterfield and his model trains would be unwelcome," the young lady said earnestly as she took Miss Beaumont's hand in hers.

"We can stay as long as you like, and I am sure that Mr Claydon has some stories about life outside of Stickleback Hollow that he has yet to tell us," Miss Beaumont replied and saw a great wave of relief wash over Lady Sarah. She settled back against the pillows on the bed and listened as the two talked for several hours.

It was almost dark by the time the doctor insisted it was time to leave. They left Lady Sarah in high spirits, and Doctor Hales led the way back to Stickleback Hollow in his own carriage to keep Mr Claydon from becoming lost in the dark.

As the trap lurched along the road, Mr Claydon tutted to himself.

"What is it, my love?" Miss Beaumont asked.

"I do not understand why anyone would gladly cause that girl pain," he said, shaking his head.

"Who do you mean?" Miss Beaumont frowned.

"Hunter, of course. Could you not see the pain written on her face when his name was mentioned? He has been avoiding her and after spending so much time with her," Mr Claydon replied.

"Perhaps there is more to it than we know," Miss Beaumont said kindly.

"Perhaps, but even so, what possible reason could there be for him to abandon her when she has been so sick?"

Mr Claydon asked.

"I suspect we shall never know, but knowing Mr Hunter, whatever his reasons, he must consider them to be good ones," Miss Beaumont shrugged.

"I have yet to meet anyone that thought their reasons for doing anything were not good ones, even the ones that are terribly flawed," Mr Claydon shook his head and sighed.

"Well, then let us hope that Mr Hunter is not flawed in his reasoning and logic," Miss Beaumont said as she squeezed the arm of Mr Claydon, very grateful that though he was a man flawed like any other, his reasoning and logic did not fail him.

Chapter 5

Arwyn and Derwyn had both been there to say goodbye to their father as he departed from Stickleback Hollow. Derwyn had been able to go back into the manor and back to his bed, but Arwyn did not have that luxury. Things had been unsettled in the village since the Berry Pickers Festival, and with the brigadier, Lady Sarah, Mrs Angela Baker, Grace, Millie, Henry Cartwright, and Captain Jonnes Smith all absent from the area, it was harder than it ordinarily would have been to return to the rhythms of everyday life.

He too had been away searching for Grace and Millie, but now he was back, the constable was determined to do what he could to help things calm down.

The first order of business was to see to any complaints that had been made in his absence that the constables from Chester had not dealt with.

There was nothing to record complaints in at the police house. Though more people than ever could read and write, the literacy rate in Stickleback Hollow was still remarkably low. This meant that in order to find out if there were complaints to deal with, Constable Evans had to walk his beat and wait for people to come to him with their problems.

He put on his thickest cloak and made sure that his boots and helmet were both buffed and clean before he stepped out of the police house.

The air was cold in the village, December was close at hand, and the first Sunday of Advent was just a day away. The first person that Constable Evans went to call on was the Reverend Percy Butterfield.

The minister was especially enthusiastic in his sermons around Christmas and Easter, but even he was less than his normal jovial self.

"Oh, constable, how good to see you. Is there any news? How fairs her ladyship?" Reverend Butterfield asked as she shook Arwyn's hand with both of his.

"She is recovering at the hospital, but it seems like she will not be home in time for Christmas," Constable Evans sighed and shook his head.

"Oh dear! How terrible for her, and what will happen

to the village tradition without her or the brigadier here? Oh dear, oh dear. What can be done about it?" the vicar asked as he released Arwyn's hand and scratched his head.

"I think that the best we can do is pray and visit Lady Sarah with smiles on our faces," the constable replied.

"Of course, of course, the Lord may yet provide us with a miracle. Indeed He already has as her ladyship yet lives. I shall redouble my efforts and take my Advent sermon to her in the hospital. That is sure to cheer her up!" the reverend clapped his hands together with glee as he fixed on his idea.

There were no problems for the constable to deal with at the church, and Arwyn was keen to escape from the reverend and his ramblings as soon as he could.

As the constable made his way around the village, it was clear that firstly there were no problems in Stickleback Hollow that needed immediate attention. Secondly, it was clear that there wasn't a soul in the village that did not know that Lady Sarah was in hospital. Nobody knew the specifics of why she was in hospital, and rumours abounded about what had happened to her and what the witch had done to her.

The rumour was far better than the truth, though Arwyn was not certain that he knew what the whole truth was, or that he wanted to know the whole truth, he was sure as long as everyone believed the wild tales they shared, Lady Sarah was safe.

It took him all morning to make his way around the village, and despite his thick cloak, the cold was seeping through to his bones. Rather than return to the police house straight away, Arwyn decided to stop at Wilson's Inn to eat lunch by a warm fireplace and take a dram of something to keep the winter chill at bay.

There were a handful of people in the Inn as Arwyn walked through the door, but there was a table right by the fire that he could take. Wilson nodded to the constable as he entered and poured out a measure of whisky to bring over to the welsh lawman.

"Lunchtime and all's well?" Wilson asked as he approached with the whisky.

"It is. All quiet in the village, save for rumours about what happened to Lady Sarah. What has Emma got cooking?" Arwyn replied as he gratefully accepted the glass of whisky.

"She's got a hot pot on the fire and some pickled red cabbage and fresh dumplings to go with it," Wilson said with a grin.

"Sounds perfect for a day like today," the constable smiled with relief.

"One hot pot coming up," Wilson nodded and swept away from the table towards the kitchen.

Emma Wilson was rarely seen outside of the kitchen when inside the inn. She worked hard creating hearty meals that would satisfy the palettes of the rich and poor alike. They were nothing fancy, but they tasted good and filled the belly.

Arwyn gazed at the fire as it danced over the wood in the fireplace and slowly sipped at the whisky. The warmth of the liquid reached deep into the core of his being and helped the fire to warm him quickly.

There were some who trusted to brandy to take away the chill of winter, but for Arwyn, whisky always seemed to do the trick.

Wilson soon returned with the dish of hot pot, the pickled cabbage and dumplings. Just as Arwyn was about to dig into the feast before him, the door to the inn was opened and Bosworth the butler, entered.

He walked straight over to where Arwyn sat and took the chair opposite.

"Bosworth, what are you doing here?" the constable frowned. It was rare that Bosworth left Grangeback Manor during the day, even when the Lord of the manor was away.

"Looking for you," Bosworth replied and waved away Wilson before the barkeep reached the table. Wilson looked a little irritated but returned to the bar with a shrug to himself.

"Why?" the constable asked mystified.

Bosworth leaned forward and glanced about to make sure no one would be close enough to hear him as he spoke. Arwyn took his first spoonful of hot pot whilst he waited for Bosworth to explain his sudden appearance.

"It's about Mr Hunter. Mrs Bosworth and Cooky have been very concerned about his behaviour as of late, but after Stanley and Lee Baker reported that Mr Hunter was visiting lots of dram houses in Chester, they went to see him at the lodge. He's terribly withdrawn and morose. The two women tried to talk some sense into him, but he didn't want to listen. Ordinarily, I wouldn't be overly concerned about leaving him to sort himself out, but something arrived today to complicate matters," Bosworth began.

"Oh?" Arwyn asked between mouthfuls.

"This arrived," Bosworth said and place an envelope on the table addressed to Lady Sarah and Mr Hunter.

"Have you not opened it?" Arwyn asked as he eyed the letter suspiciously.

"Yes. The brigadier and the others are coming home soon. There are some other details, but we do not know when the brigadier will appear. There is no date in the letter. If he returns before Lady Sarah has left the hospital and before Mr Hunter has recovered his composure, I don't know what will happen," Bosworth said with concern.

"Why would Hunter being in a sullen state and Lady Sarah in hospital be a problem for the brigadier when he returns?" Arwyn frowned.

"Because it will be his daughter all over again. He will not lose another child and survive it. Both Mr Hunter and Lady Sarah are as important as Miss Lucy was. There is nothing that can be done to hurry Lady Sarah's return, but will you go to see Mr Hunter? Talk to him?" Bosworth pleaded.

"I will," Arwyn nodded with a heavy sigh. He looked down at his food and resolved that though talking to Hunter was important, it could wait until after he had finished his lunch.

Chapter 6

Stanley and Lee Baker were in the guardianship of Lady Sarah, and the household of Grangeback whilst their mother was away with the brigadier.

The two boys had taken quite a shine to Mr Hunter and had spent most of their days following the groundskeeper around, learning about the woods, developing the skills they would need as hunters, and when they were not outdoors, they could be found in the kitchen at Grangeback, begging for food.

Yet with the change in Mr Hunter's demeanour, there had been a growing concern about the influence that Mr Hunter would exert over the two young boys, and what kind of example he was setting.

When Lee and Stanley had followed Mr Hunter to Chester and witnessed his tour of the dram shops, neither had understood what it meant, nor what a bad example it was for them.

However, when they returned to Stickleback Hollow,

and Cooky asked what they had done with their day, the seriousness of the matter had not been lost on her.

She had listened with a smile on her face, the one she reserved for humouring children when they talked of adventures and tall tales, but did not betray the emotions that were hidden beneath it.

After the two boys had finished relating their day in full, Cooky made sure they were fed and sent them off to the stables to see if they could help the grooms at all. With Lady Sarah in hospital and Mr Hunter drinking himself into a daily stupor, their horses, Harald and Black Guy, were being exercised by the grooms, meaning they had less time to take care of their chores.

Though they could not be trusted to clean the leather tack, they could muck out the stables easily enough, and it was an excuse to force the boys to bathe every night, something they were not used to living with their mother.

When Stanley and Lee had scampered off to the stables, Cooky had abandoned the dinner preparations for the rest of the household and gone in search of Mrs Bosworth.

There had been no question that the housekeeper

needed to be informed of what Cooky had just heard, and though the foul mood of Mrs Bosworth made her a terror to approach, Cooky was counting on using that temper to help change their current of affairs.

Things, however, had not worked out as Cooky had hoped. Though Mrs Bosworth reacted the way Cooky expected and the pair had gone to confront Mr Hunter, he had proven to be little better to talk to than a brick wall.

On their walk back from their visit to Mr Hunter, Cooky had thought about what to do about Stanley and Lee Baker living in the manor with Mr Hunter so close at hand. She thought for a few days and could only see one possible way to protect the boys.

At breakfast on the third day, Doctor Hales was alone at the breakfast table. Now that Edryd had departed, Derwyn was almost constantly in the company of Miss DeVille, and Mr Hunter was imbibing a liquid diet, he was considering relocating back to his home.

"Doctor, may I talk to you?" Cooky asked as she tentatively opened the door to the dining room.

"Of course, Cooky, come sit down. It is extremely lonely eating by one's self," Jack Hales replied.

"Thank you," Cooky smiled weakly and sat on the chair to the doctor's right.

"So, what can an ageing physician do for the best cook in the county, if not the country?" the doctor asked brightly between mouthfuls of eggs.

"I would like to know if you would take Stanley and Lee Baker back to your house to stay until either Lady Sarah returns, or Miss Baker does," Cooky said in a single breath.

The doctor frowned slightly and leaned back in his chair.

"I will admit, I had considered taking the two boys with me, but I didn't know you were so concerned about them," the doctor replied as he looked at Cooky with a steady gaze.

"Sir, the boys are wonderful, and it has been a pleasure to have them here, but I am worried about the example Mr Hunter is setting. I think a little distance from him would be best for them all," Cooky sighed sadly.

"I see, very well. They should be down to eat any moment, I will tell them that they are coming to stay with me for a few days whilst Mrs Bosworth had their rooms cleaned," Jack agreed, and Cooky smiled gratefully.

"Thank you, doctor. Now, I must be getting back to the kitchen," she said, stood and bustled from the room in a much happier mood than the one she had entered in.

As the door to the dining room closed behind Cooky, the doctor could hear footsteps thundering down the corridor above him, then down the stairs. A few moments later, the door to the dining room was flung open, and Stanley and Lee Baker rushed in.

"Good morning," the doctor said brightly.

"Mornin'," the two boys chorused as they piled their plates with food and sat down to inhale the food.

"I have some news for you both. You are going to come to my house for a few days. Mrs Bosworth needs to clean our rooms, so we'll need to be elsewhere," the doctor announced.

Neither Stanley nor Lee Baker had ever lived in a house where someone was paid to clean everything for them. To them, it sounded reasonable that Mrs Bosworth would need them to be out of the house to clean everything properly as their rooms were bigger than their mother's house and shop combined.

"When you've finished, erm, eating, you will need to

pack your things. Then we will depart for my lodgings. You'll still have your own rooms, but they won't be quite as grand as your rooms here," Doctor Hales smiled at the two boys.

At their own home, they shared a small room that had room for nothing more than two straw sacks thrown on wooden frames with a single blanket over each and a small fire grate that stood between the two beds. Though not the luxuries that were enjoyed by those at Grangeback or even at the doctor's house, they both knew how lucky they were compared to most other children of their age.

"Sir, could we ask you somethin'?" Lee asked between mouthfuls.

"Of course you may," the doctor said kindly.

"Can we go see Lady Sarah? It's been very strange without her in the house. We know she's very ill, but can we just see her for a moment?" Stanley asked with hope shining brightly in his eyes.

"I am sure she would be overjoyed to see you both. We can go as soon as we have taken your things to my house," the doctor announced, and the two boys couldn't help but grin.

Though the doctor, did not think it was possible, the two boys ate even faster than before, finishing their mounds of breakfast food before the doctor and darting off to pack their belongings.

Within the hour, the two boys and the doctor had taken their leave of Grangeback, Jack Hales sure to loudly tell Mrs Bosworth that they would be back as soon as the rooms had been cleaned. The doctor was sure that Cooky would have spoken to Mrs Bosworth but doubted the rest of the staff would have been told.

His loud announcement served to tell the rest of the household that the boys would be back soon enough and left everyone feeling a little brighter at the prospect of their departure.

The doctor took his small coach to the hospital, and it was big enough for the two boys and the doctor to sit in comfortably.

With the three of them bundled into the coach, they set off for the hospital. There was a lot for the two boys to look at from the coach, and they seemed to enjoy the journey.

As they disembarked from the coach at the hospital, Lee Baker pulled something from the floor of the coach and hid it quickly behind his back.

"What have you got there?" the doctor frowned and gripping Lee by the shoulder turned him to reveal a bunch of flowers concealed behind his back.

"They're for Lady Sarah," Stanley said with an embarrassed air as the cheeks of the two boys went bright red.

"Where did you get them from?" the doctor asked with surprise.

"From the garden at Grangeback. They're her flowers, she should get to see some of them," Lee stammered.

The doctor smiled at the two boys and shook his head.

"Though I am sure Mrs Bosworth will not be happy to see you have taken them, it was a lovely thought."

The doctor led the way into the hospital, and the nosy nurse at the desk didn't dare challenge him or the two boys as they walked by.

Doctor Hales stopped at the door to Lady Sarah's room and knocked.

"Come in," Lady Sarah's voice sounded from within, and the two Baker boys took a deep breath as the doctor opened the door.

"I've brought you a waif and a stray to visit," the doctor grinned as the two boys stood in the doorway, staring at her ladyship.

Lady Sarah smiled broadly at them and held out her arms to the boys. It was all the prompting that Lee and Stanley needed to rush forwards and throw themselves at her. The flowers flew into her lap as the two boys wrapped their arms around her neck and held on tightly.

Lady Sarah fought back tears as the love the two boys felt for her overwhelmed her. She held each with one arm until they were ready to let go.

"We brung you flowers from your garden," Lee said as he picked up the flowers off the bed and held them out to Lady Sarah.

"Oh, how beautiful, thank you both," she replied as she took the flowers from Lee and breathed in the scent of the blossoms.

"You look much better today," the doctor said, sensing that Lady Sarah was going to cry. The two Baker boys fought over the small chair next to the bed until they both managed to squeeze onto it.

"I feel much better. Hopefully, it will not be too long until I am ready to leave," Lady Sarah replied brightly.

"Good, good, I hope you are not too bored here on your own," the doctor said as he took the flowers from Lady Sarah and looked around for a suitable vessel to display them in. He settled on a glass of water that was sat beside the bed.

"No, I was, to begin with, but there seems to be something of a mystery in this hospital," Lady Sarah replied.

"Oh? You do have a habit of discovering mysteries wherever you go," the doctor chuckled.

"That may be so, but this one is especially mysterious. There are rumours that people are disappearing from the hospital. All of them are people that nobody visits and some of them are said to be those that should be in sanatoriums but for whatever reason have ended up here," Lady Sarah explained.

"Well, perhaps this is one mystery that has a logical explanation. I will talk to the nurses and see if I can't find out what is happening to these people that are supposedly disappearing," the doctor replied.

Chapter 7

When Cooky and Mrs Bosworth had left the lodge, Pattinson had stayed with his master. The dog has missed the giant hunter and as much fun as Pattinson had being fed by the cook and servants at Grangeback, he had wanted to go back to his home with Alex.

The Akita knew that his master was unhappy and lay beside him on the floor of the lodge, his head in the lap of the hunter.

Alex had not moved since Cooky, and Mrs Bosworth had left - at least to Mr Hunter it felt like he hadn't moved. In reality, he had moved a great deal over the few days, but he had always made his way back to the floor by the fire.

Pattinson had followed his master wherever he went and had not whined or barked once, even when Mr Hunter forgot to feed him.

Though he absently stroked the Japanese hunting dog, Alex was barely aware of Pattinson's presence beside him. His mind was whirling with all the emotions he felt, and his thoughts of loss soon led him to the loss of his mother.

Before his mother had died, Mr Hunter had been a happy child, he wanted for nothing. He had a loving home, plenty of fresh air and a groundskeeper that was happy to indulge the whims of a young boy that was interested in nature.

But when his mother had died, he had been left with a wound that had never fully healed. It was a sucking wound that had robbed him of all happiness and had caused him no small amount of physical and emotional pain.

He had no way of escaping it, wherever he went, the pain was there. Nothing could distract him from it either. Mrs Bosworth and Cooky had done their best to comfort the boy, but nothing they said or did, made things any better for Alex. In fact, their attempts to help him had been taken as them trying to replace his mother.

The brigadier had been lost in his own grief and barely noticed the pain the little boy of the lodge was suffering. George Webb-Kneelingroach had done his best to avoid Mr Hunter in the days that had followed not only Alex's mother's death but the death of the brigadier's wife as well.

It was not long after the two women had died that the brigadier had decided to send MrHunter to boarding school. Though it was important that the young boy received a good education, it seemed to Alex that the brigadier had sent him away to remove him from his home and lands.

The more he had thought about his father over the last few days and how the brigadier had reacted to the death of Alex's mother and his wife, Mr Hunter had become more convinced that the brigadier had been trying to get rid of him.

His pretence that he wanted to provide a young boy with nothing with an education that could help him in his life and society. Sending the boy away to a school that would keep him there, even during the school holidays if required. Not even acknowledging his son in the privacy of the society Stickleback Hollow when his wife and daughter were both dead and only his own pride could be hurt by the admission. Treating Lady Sarah with far more respect and consideration than he had ever shown to him.

Every time the face of the brigadier floated across Alex's mind, a new slight appeared with it. Something that the brigadier had done or not done that showed how little he cared for his son. How little the happiness of Mr Hunter matter.

He had known happiness as a boy with his mother, and as a man with Lady Sarah. But he had lost his mother and now he had lost Lady Sarah.

As far as Mr Hunter was concerned, there was only one man responsible for the loss of his mother, the loss of Lady Sarah and for the sadness, bitterness and suffering that Mr Hunter had endured throughout his life. And that man was Brigadier George Webb-Kneelingroach.

Chapter 8

Stanley and Lee Baker were in no hurry to leave the hospital or the company of Lady Sarah. They had stories of their adventures around Stickleback Hollow to regale her with, and Lady Sarah never got tired of listening to the two boys.

This allowed Doctor Hales to slip away to investigate the little mystery that Lady Sarah had reported. Though Lady Sarah did have a habit of finding trouble wherever she went, there was something about the rumours that left the doctor feeling unsettled.

There had been a recent influx of patients into the hospital, and the doctor had not seen the records of all of them. There had been some that had come from the asylum, but most had been people that had walked in off the street, so to speak.

The files of each patient were kept in a small office that was run by a clerk, who was overworked and extremely underpaid for the work they did.

It was rare that the doctor visited the records room, save to drop off some paperwork when the nurses were too busy to do it.

The clerk always appeared to be flustered by the volume of paperwork that was generated by the hospital staff and how he was supposed to be keeping it organised.

Not only was the clerk taxed with keeping all of the records for the hospital in order, but he was also responsible for keeping track of all the payments for the patients' treatment.

There was clearly more work than one man could handle, but the records office was not big enough for more than one person to work in, and the clerk was too proud to ask for any help.

As a result, he often prioritised the payment paperwork over the organisation of the patients' paperwork. Not only was it left by the wayside because there was too much for the clerk to do, but also because it was rare for a doctor to need to check any of the records kept in the record room.

So it was a great surprise to the clerk when Doctor Hales knocked on his door, interested in collecting the paperwork of the most recent patients in the hospital.

"If you aren't their doctor, I'm not sure that you are allowed to take their records," the clerk frowned as he leaned back in his chair and rubbed the top of his nose.

A groove had been worn into his nose by his spectacles, and the clerk often found that the two marks throbbed when he was feeling stressed and pressured.

Doctor Hales asking for medical records for a number of patients would only lead to trouble as far as the clerk was concerned, and trouble was something that the clerk wanted to avoid at all costs.

"I will look at and take whatever records I please. If a doctor has been doing something they shouldn't, I am not the sort of chap to look the other way," the doctor sneered at the clerk. He doubted very much that any of the doctors had bribed the clerk into keeping hold of the records he wanted, but it never hurt to imply that the clerk was complicit in a conspiracy if only to ensure co-operation.

The clerk blushed a deep crimson at the insinuation, then obediently went about searching for the records that Doctor Hales wanted.

He watched for nearly half an hour as the clerk

searched through piles of paper that seemed to be flung any which way he pleased, pulling out the odd piece every now and then until he had a small stack to present to the doctor.

"Thank you," the doctor said dryly, making a mental note that something had to be done about the clerk and the state of the records room. But for now, he had a pile of papers to focus on. He carried the stack through the hospital to his office. He then sat in his high-backed chair, made sure the door was closed and began to read.

As he went through the papers, he discovered something startling. It was not that anyone was missing, at least as far as he could tell from the paperwork. It was how inaccurate and incomplete the records were. Even looking at the papers that related to Lady Sarah showed the doctor that someone was not doing their job.

The more he read, the more he was certain that either someone was being lazy, or that someone was neglecting their paperwork on purpose.

From what he had in front of him, it was clear to the doctor that if he did not know Lady Sarah was in the hospital, he would have no idea what was wrong with her, what room she was in, or indeed if she was still a patient or not.

The same was true of at least seven of the other patients that he had paperwork for.

He put down the papers and checked his watch. He had left Lady Sarah and the Baker boys for nearly an hour now. Jack felt like it was time to go back and take the boys home, but he didn't want to leave the issue of the paperwork alone.

After checking his watch again, he resolved that he had a little time still in which he could talk to the nurse that was supposed to be in charge of checking the papers before they were filed. He had to be quick though, as he knew that Lady Sarah needed her rest.

He took Lady Sarah's paperwork with him, leaving the rest in his office, locking the door behind him. He walked swiftly down the corridors until he reached the desk at the front of the hospital where the nurse sat.

Her name was Bryony Smith, and the doctor was not surprised that the same nurse that had caused problems for Miss Beaumont and Mr Claydon, was the one that was responsible for the shoddy paperwork.

"Can you please explain to my why this paperwork is

incomplete and has been filed?" the doctor demanded as he pushed the papers under the nurse's nose.

"I'm sorry, doctor, but it's nothing to do with me," the nurse replied with a shrug.

"Sadly, that is not true. You are the nurse responsible for checking all paperwork before it is filed, are you not?" the doctor demanded.

"I was, sir, but not anymore. The new doctor decided that it shouldn't be a nurse's job. He took the task away from me when he arrived a month ago. Perhaps you should go and talk to him if there is a problem," the nurse replied, her smugness barely concealed by her smile.

"And which doctor is supposedly now in charge of checking paperwork?" the doctor narrowed his eyes at Nurse Smith.

"Doctor Marcus Duckett, I'll take you to him," Bryony replied and beckoned for Doctor Hales to follow her.

Chapter 9

The front desk was vacant when Derwyn and Miss DeVille arrived at the hospital. Miss DeVille was somewhat relieved to find there was no nurse at the desk. Miss Beaumont had related the details of their visit in full to the pair, and Miss DeVille had been quite nervous at the prospect of having to argue her way into the hospital.

Miss Beaumont had also made sure that the pair knew how to get to Lady Sarah's room before they left Stickleback Hollow.

"If the doctor isn't there, then you will have to find your own way," Miss Beaumont had warned them, having no faith in Nurse Smith's ability to be helpful.

Derwyn was glad that Miss Beaumont had been so insistent with her instructions. The hospital corridors seemed like a maze to the Welshman, and he was certain that they would have become hopelessly lost in moments if they had not been given such detailed direction.

Miss DeVille was the first to reach the door to Lady

Sarah's room and was surprised to find that it was open and that her ladyship already had visitors.

The two Baker boys were still talking animatedly to the lady, though Lady Sarah seemed to be close to falling asleep.

She was leaning back on her pillows, a contented smile on her face and her eyelids drooping.

"What's all this noise then?" Derwyn asked in a teasing voice as he stepped into the room. Miss DeVille hoovered outside the door, unsure if she should enter.

Lady Sarah turned her head, her smile broadening as she made to welcome her new visitors.

"Miss DeVille, Mr Evans, how kind of you to come," Lady Sarah said in a slightly quieter voice than she would have normally used.

"We thought that you might be in need of some company, but it seems that young Lee and Stanley have beaten us to it!" Derwyn said as he approached the two Baker boys and tousled their hair.

"We're sorry, your ladyship, we shouldn't have come. We should go and let you rest," Miss DeVille said in a small voice from the doorway.

"Not at all, come and tell me your news," Lady Sarah gave Miss DeVille a small smile as she closed her eyes and listened to the Baker boys chattering to Derwyn, and Miss DeVille telling of all the things that she and Derwyn had done since Lady Sarah had come to the hospital.

Though Lady Sarah was exhausted from having so many people visit her all at once, it made her feel happier than she had felt in weeks.

The only thing that she was truly missing whilst she was restricted to the bed in the small hospital room was Mr Hunter. She did not ask about him or why he had not been to visit her. The truth about his absence was not something that she wanted to hear about from anyone for fear of how much it would hurt her.

His lack of presence, though painful, was bearable. Knowing that he simply no longer cared enough to visit her would be too much for her heart, already breaking from the loss of their child.

"Did you happen to see Doctor Hales as you came in?" Lady Sarah asked when Miss DeVille had finished sharing her news.

"No, in fact, we didn't see anyone at all between the

hospital entrance and your room," Miss DeVille replied.

"How strange," Lady Sarah frowned.

"Why? Is there something you need from him?" Derwyn asked.

"He went to check on some records, but that was nearly two hours ago. I don't know where he could be. He brought Stanley and Lee with him, and I am not sure how they will get home again if he does not come back soon," Lady Sarah replied, looking with some concern at the two boys.

There was only so much time that two young boys could find sitting in a hospital entertaining. The excitement of seeing Lady Sarah and the arrival of Derwyn and Miss DeVille had been pleasant enough distractions, but it was clear that the Baker boys wanted to go home.

"We can take the boys back to the manor," Derwyn volunteered.

"Thank you, I do not want them to be stranded here for hours," Lady Sarah smiled with relief.

"Is there anything else that you need?" Miss DeVille asked as she rose to her feet and looked down at bed-bound lady.

"Could you ask Constable Evans and Mr Hunter to come this evening, please? There is something I need from them both," Lady Sarah said with a deep sigh.

She did not want to show any emotion when she mentioned Alex's name, but her voice wavered slightly. She wanted to see him desperately, but at the same time, she did not want to see him at all if he was only going to break her heart further.

Yet, if there was a mystery that lurked in the hospital, she needed the help of both Arwyn and Alex. The length of time that Doctor Hales had been gone made her nervous, and even more certain that there was something nefarious afoot.

"Constable Evans will certainly be willing to come, my lady. Derwyn, could you take the boys to the coach you borrowed from Grangeback? Ask the driver to prepare for our departure?" Miss DeVille said with a kind smile. Derwyn nodded and said farewell to Lady Sarah. Lee and Stanley waved goodbye and followed Derwyn from the hospital room.

Miss DeVille closed the door behind them. When she was sure that they were out of earshot, she sat back down beside Lady Sarah.

"What is wrong?" Lady Sarah asked with worry.

"Mr Hunter has turned to drink. I do not know how much Lee and Stanley know, but the idolise the man, and I do not want to speak ill of him in front of them. He is said to have locked himself in the brigadier's study at first, and now he is locked in the lodge. I do not know if anything that we say can make him unlock the door, but we will try," Miss DeVille said sadly.

"I see. Thank you," Lady Sarah said, biting her lip so that she would not cry.

"We will come and see you again. Take care," Miss DeVille said and left Lady Sarah alone in her room.

The moment that Miss DeVille had closed the door behind her, Lady Sarah burst into tears and sobbed into her hands. Things were far worse than she had feared.

Chapter 10

It felt strange to Constable Evans as he made his way to the lodge. He had grown into his role as a policeman over the last few years and had become comfortable with upholding the law in order to protect the people of Stickleback Hollow.

However, this was the first time that he had to approach a friend and confront them about something personal. If it had not been for Bosworth's entreating, Arwyn would have happily left Mr Hunter to wallow in his self-pity.

It was not something that he would have done out of malice, but more out of an unwillingness to interfere in the business or lives of other people.

There was a certain degree of intrusion that accompanied his day job, but he was always careful to not overstep his bounds as a policeman. Nor was he one to gossip with other people over a pint at Wilson's Inn.

If a friend came and asked him for help on a specific matter, he was always happy to give it, but he wouldn't dream of wading into a situation because he decided that help was needed.

So as he made the journey from Stickleback Hollow to the lodge that Mr Hunter called home, he tried to overcome the uncomfortable feeling in his belly.

Arwyn had done his best to stay out of Mr Hunter's way in recent days as well. He had no desire to be used as a go-between by the groundskeeper and did not want to report on Lady Sarah's condition, happiness or lack thereof when Mr Hunter should be the one visiting her.

The constable was not happy with Mr Hunter's conduct, but unlike Cooky and Mrs Bosworth, he was not prepared to openly judge the hunter.

By the time that Arwyn reached the lodge and reached up to knock on the door, he was no closer to reconciling with the role he had to fulfil.

He knocked three times. The sound of it echoed through the silence of the forest and resounded through the seemingly empty rooms of the lodge.

Pattinson barked in reply to the knock and rushed to scratch at the door. But there were no sounds of Mr Hunter stirring inside.

Arwyn knocked again, and again until he finally heard the clattering of bottles over the sound of Pattinson barking and the lumbering, heavy footsteps of Mr Hunter approaching the door.

"Mrs Bosworth, Cooky, I have no desire to -" Alex began as he opened the door, but stopped mid-sentence when he saw Arwyn standing on his doorstep.

"Hunter," Arwyn said gruffly.

"Evans, why are you here?" Alex frowned at his friend.

"Bosworth sent me to talk you," Constable Evans replied.

"You mean Mrs Bosworth sent you," Mr Hunter said coldly.

"No, Bosworth came to find me. Everyone is worried about you. You need to talk to someone about what is going on," Arwyn sighed as Pattinson jumped around the constable.

The distraction of the dog desiring attention was enough to help ease the uncomfortable tension that was hanging in the air. Constable Evans knelt down to fuss the dog as he thought of what to say next.

"I don't need to talk to anyone," Alex shrugged and tried to shut the door.

Pattinson growled and pushed against the door to keep it open.

"Hunter, the brigadier is coming home. Whatever business has kept him away is finished. Do you want him to see you like this when he gets home?" Arwyn asked as he put his hand on the door to stop Alex from closing it.

"I don't care how he sees me," Mr Hunter sneered.

"You don't mean that," Arwyn said with shock. He'd known Mr Hunter for many years. Even when he had been at his gruffest and had kept his distance from the other people of Stickleback Hollow, he had still harboured a great deal of love and respect for the brigadier.

"I don't? How would you know that? Everything in my life that has gone wrong, every terrible thing is down to him. Why would I care what he thinks of me?" Mr Hunter asked as he levelled a hard stare at Arwyn.

"Because out of everyone in this world, there are only two people who have shown you unconditional love and respect. The brigadier is one of them. The other is sat in a hospital bed wondering what she could possibly have done in order to be cast aside and ignored so easily," Constable Evans barely kept control of his temper as he spoke. He had not imagined that he would find Mr Hunter in such a bad way.

"Don't talk to me about her!" Alex shouted at Arwyn and took a step towards the constable, trying to intimidate him. Constable Evans didn't flinch, he simply stared back at the hunter.

"Then go see her," Arwyn replied icily.

"No, I won't be welcome. I'm sorry, Evans," Alex said, shaking his head, "There's a lot to all this you won't understand. But if you could take Pattinson for a few days for me, I would appreciate it. I have things that I need to take care of," Mr Hunter said as his mood switched from aggressive to melancholy.

"Of course. You do have friends you can talk to, you know. Whenever you are ready," Arwyn said. Alex nodded absent-mindedly and slowly shut the door, leaving Pattinson whining, wanting to go back to his master.

"Come, Pattinson, we need to go for a walk," Constable Evans said brightly, causing Pattinson to bark excitedly. The constable turned away from the door and began walking towards Stickleback Hollow, the dog bounding ahead of him, sniffing every tree that he could find.

Mr Hunter's mood swings and general attitude were worrying enough, but when Alex had given Pattinson to Arwyn to care for, alarm bells had begun ringing in Arwyn's brain.

He was certain that there must be someone in Stickleback Hollow that Alex would listen to, that could reach through the darkness that Mr Hunter had surrounded himself with and pull him back to the light.

Though Lady Sarah was the first person that sprang to mind, there was one other person that Arwyn thought that he could call upon to help - the Reverend Percy Butterfield.

As he reached the path that led towards the church, Arwyn headed up it, hoping to find the vicar alone in the building.

It was cool and dark by the time that Arwyn reached the church. The evenings were getting longer as the days got shorter, but the constable knew his way to the church, even in the dark.

He reached the door of the church and found it open. Inside, the reverend was lighting candles and singing carols to himself as he worked. Pattinson barked to announce their arrival.

"Ah Constable, Pattinson, what a pleasant surprise!" Percy Butterfield beamed as he put out the taper he was using and turned his attention to the policeman.

"Perhaps not as pleasant as you think," Arwyn sighed.

"Oh? Come, let us have some tea and tiffin, that should make any situation a little more civil," the reverend smiled and beckoned for Arwyn to follow him to the vicarage.

The pair walked in silence, Pattinson trotting happily along, enjoying the cool evening air. The two men remained silent as they entered the house, water was boiled, tea was brewed, and cake was brought out.

It was only after his first sip of tea and bite of cake that the silence was broken by Constable Evans.

"I'm sorry, reverend, but I need your help," he sighed.

Chapter 11

The conversation with Reverend Percy Butterfield lasted for several hours. The reverend had listened to what Arwyn had observed, what had happened during his visit to Mr Hunter, what Bosworth had said, and every conversation that Arwyn had with anyone in the last few weeks regarding Mr Hunter.

When Arwyn was finished, the reverend had asked several questions, then sat in silence for a while. He thought things over but kept any conclusions he had arrived at to himself.

Eventually, he had agreed to go visit Mr Hunter and to see what he could do to help the groundskeeper. Arwyn had left the vicarage feeling relieved, though he knew that nothing was resolved just yet. The reverend was a man of God, and as far as the constable could see it would take a miracle to bring Alex back from the brink he had pushed himself to.

By the time he reached the village of Stickleback

Hollow proper, his stomach was growling and so was Pattinson's. Rather than walking back to the police house to make food for both of them, he decided to pay a visit to Wilson's Inn for the second time that day.

As he walked through the door, Wilson waved him over.

"I have some interesting news for you," Wilson said with a wry smile as Arwyn approached the bar.

"Oh? What?" the constable asked as he watched Wilson pouring him a pint.

"Duffleton Hall has just been bought. After all the terrible things that have happened, I was beginning to think the place was cursed and it would stand empty forever," Wilson said as he put the full glass of beer down on the bar.

"Do you know who bought it?" Arwyn asked with surprise.

"Apparently a Doctor Marcus Duckett. Rumour is he wants to open some form of sanatorium there for the incredibly rich," Wilson replied.

"All those rich relatives visiting, be very good for business," Arwyn grinned at the innkeeper.

"The thought never crossed my mind!" Wilson

laughed and winked at the constable.

It felt good to share a joke with someone after the day that Arwyn had.

"Are you eating here?" Wilson asked.

"Yes, and I'll need something for Pattinson too," Arwyn replied.

"Oh? Hunter given him up?" Wilson frowned.

"No, he's got business to attend to. Asked me to look after him for a few days," the constable replied in an offhand manner, trying to deflect any further questions.

"Well, then Pattinson shall have his dinner too. I'll go see what Emma can whip up for you," Wilson said as he disappeared into the kitchen.

Arwyn made his way to one of the tables in the far corner of the inn, close to the fire, but with enough space for the dog to lie down by the wall without behind in the way of other patrons.

It didn't take long for Wilson to bring out a small feast for the constable and the dog, which was devoured almost as quickly as it had appeared.

Arwyn leant back in his chair and sighed contentedly, beginning to think of his bed and an early night. The door to the inn swung open, and Miss DeVille entered. She looked around the room until she spied the constable and made her way over to him.

Arwyn inwardly groaned to himself as he realised that his bed was going to have to wait.

"Miss DeVille, what can I do for you?" the constable asked, trying not to show the irritation he felt.

"I'm sorry to bother you, constable, but Lady Sarah needs you and Mr Hunter at the hospital," Miss DeVille said in a hushed voice.

"Both of us?" Arwyn frowned.

"Yes, that's what she said. I think it has something to do with Doctor Hales and a mystery. Derwyn has gone to tell Mr Hunter after he has dropped the Baker boys off at Grangeback," Miss DeVille replied.

"I thought the boys were staying with the doctor for a while," the constable said with growing concern.

"I don't know what is happening, but Lady Sarah did seem very worried," Miss DeVille shrugged.

"Very well, let us walk you home and then we will head to the hospital," Arwyn said as he rose to his feet and tried to rally his mind for the journey to the hospital and whatever waited for him there.

Chapter 12

Derwyn had asked the driver of the coach to head to Grangeback after they dropped Miss DeVille at the gate to the police house. He intended to take Lee and Stanley Baker back to the manor before he went to fetch Mr Hunter, but the two boys had other plans.

They pleaded and moaned until Derwyn relented and wearily agreed that they could come to the lodge too. The driver chuckled to himself at how the two Baker boys had the ability to get whatever they wanted out of most of the residents of Stickleback Hollow.

The road did not go as far as the lodge. When the house had first been built, the road had gone right past the lodge, but as the forest and gardens had been shaped and changed over the years, the lodge was now surrounded by trees and often difficult to find for those who had not visited the estate before.

The driver pulled up on the road and bid the trio goodnight. The lodge was walking distance from Grangeback

Manor, and there was no need to keep the driver or the horses from their beds.

Derwyn made sure that the two Baker boys were sensible enough to know not to run off ahead of him before they set off into the trees. As they began to make their way through the woods to the lodge, they heard the faint sound of the Reverend Percy Butterfield's voice drifting through the trees.

"Please, Alexander, open the door," the vicar begged as he shouted at the door.

"Reverend, what's going on?" Derwyn frowned as he, Stanley and Lee, approached.

"Mr Hunter has locked his door and is refusing to leave the lodge. I was asked to come and speak with him by Constable Evans. There is a great deal of sorrow and darkness in his heart, but if he does not open this door, there is not much any of us can do to help!" Percy directed the last comment towards the door. It was clear to Derwyn that the clergyman was close to losing his temper.

There were several things that Derwyn had learned about the reverend during his time in Stickleback Hollow. 1) He had a love of cricket and steam engines that was unrivalled by any man that Derwyn had ever met. 2) He was a man that could be counted on to provide comfort and support in a time for need. 3) His Sunday sermons were often fifteen minutes too long. 4) He was more patient than anyone Derwyn had known.

To see the vicar so close to losing his temper with Mr Hunter told Derwyn that Alex was in a far worse place than the Welshman had originally thought. To not visit Lady Sarah and to avoid the company of the occupants of Grangeback had been easy to dismiss as the behaviours of a man dealing with his own grief, but to frustrate Percy Butterfield, man of God, was a sign of a desperate situation.

Derwyn looked down at the Baker boys and wished that he had taken them back to Grangeback before he had come. But there was nothing to be done now.

"How long have you been trying to talk with him?" Derwyn asked.

"At least an hour, probably much more. My throat is hoarse, and I am in need of my supper. But there is a man behind this door who needs help and as long as I can speak and stand, I will not abandon him," the reverend said firmly.

Derwyn hoped that Alex had heard the old man's

words and that the door would open momentarily, but nothing stirred in the lodge.

"Mr Hunter, it's Derwyn, Arwyn's brother," Derwyn said as he stepped past the vicar and banged on the door with his large fist.

"Did your brother send you too?" Alex asked with contempt.

"No. Lady Sarah sent me," Derwyn said coldly. The sound of glass bottles crashing on the floor was the only reply that Derwyn received, but the sound let him know that Alex had some form of reaction to the statement.

"Don't speak lies to me," Mr Hunter eventually replied when the cascade of bottle crashes had finished.

"I haven't lied to you as long as I've known you, and I'm not about to start now. Miss DeVille and I went to visit her at the hospital. She asked for you and Constable Evans to come to her. Miss DeVille went to fetch the constable, and I have come for you," Derwyn said gruffly.

"And why should I go?" Alex asked, his voice held an edge of anxiety.

"Because the lady is asking for you," Derwyn replied firmly.

"Unlock the door, Alexander, Lady Sarah needs you. Now is the time to leave the lodge and go to her," the reverend urged.

Silence was the reply. It extended for what felt like an eternity until Mr Hunter finally spoke.

"No. She has no need of me. And it is not your place to tell me where I should go and when," Mr Hunter said morosely.

"How can you say that?" Lee Baker exploded. The young boy had been listening to the three adults, getting more upset with every passing moment until he could no longer contain himself.

"Who is that?" Mr Hunter asked with concern.

"It's Lee and Stanley, you coward!" Stanley shouted, just as distressed as his brother was.

"Yes! Coward! You won't go to the hospital to see Lady Sarah because you are scared!" Lee yelled.

"We saw you buying all those bottles. You're just sat getting drunk whilst Lady Sarah is all alone at the hospital. You're a coward, and I hate you!" Stanley shouted.

"I hate you more!" Lee yelled and picked by a stone and threw it at the door. The two boys burst into tears the moment the rock left Lee's hand, and the pair turned and ran in the direction of Grangeback.

"It is a sad thing when we lose our heroes," Percy Butterfield sighed and shook his head sadly.

"I hope you can live with your choices, Hunter, I really hope you can," Derwyn said through the door before he said his goodbye to the reverend and went after the two Baker boys.

Chapter 18

Constable Evans did not wait for Mr Hunter. As soon as Miss DeVille told him that Lady Sarah had requested his presence, he set off for the hospital.

The later in the day it was, the harder it was to reach the hospital for the constable. The light on the roads from Stickleback Hollow to the city was very poor, and the lantern that hung from the police wagon cast a small radius of light that meant that Arwyn could see only a few feet in front of the horses' noses. This meant that he couldn't see very far up the road in the dark.

Moving quickly on the roads in those conditions was not only foolish but dangerous. After the carriage accident that had killed the brigadier's wife and Mr Hunter's mother, none of those in Stickleback Hollow had taken any unnecessary risks when it came to travelling.

Though his progress was not quick, he arrived at the hospital sooner than Lady Sarah expected him to. None of the staff stopped the policeman as he made his way down the halls.

He paused briefly to knock on the closed door and waited for permission to enter.

"Come in," the anxious voice of Lady Sarah could barely be heard through the door. "Arwyn, I am so glad you are here!" Lady Sarah cried as he entered her room.

"You sent for me? Miss DeVille could not tell me very much, but I did not think it sounded as though it could wait until tomorrow," Constable Evans replied.

"Doctor Hales went to investigate the disappearances that are rumoured to try and calm any suspicions I have, but he has been gone for several hours. I have tried to get out of this bed and look for him, but as soon as I am seen, I am ushered back into this room," Lady Sarah sighed with frustration.

"What disappearances? Miss DeVille only mentioned Doctor Hales and mystery," Arwyn said as he shut the door before moving to sit down beside Lady Sarah's bed.

"There are a number of patients that have gone missing from the hospital over the last few weeks and months. I don't know how long this has been happening, but there have been a number of them in the last week. They are all patients that nobody comes to visit or those that should be in a sanatorium instead of a hospital like this," Lady Sarah explained as she kept glancing towards the door.

As Constable Evans had arrived, she had hoped that Mr Hunter would not be far behind.

"And the doctor went to look into these disappearances?" Arwyn asked.

"He went to look at the records to see if any patients have gone missing. He was certain there was nothing to the rumours, but the longer he is gone, the more convinced I am that there is more to the rumours than there first appeared to be," Lady Sarah said earnestly.

"And you are certain that the doctor hasn't been called away and forgot to come back to you?" Arwyn asked as tactfully as he could. Lady Sarah had a very sharp mind, and the constable wasn't entirely convinced that she was not creating a mystery to keep herself from losing her sanity whilst confined to the small room.

"If that were the case, then he willfully abandoned Lee and Stanley Baker," Lady Sarah replied testily.

"I see. Then I will go and see what I can find out about his whereabouts," Constable Evans said, feeling slightly sheepish.

"Please hurry back," Lady Sarah said anxiously.

"I do not think that you should be left alone though," Constable Evans replied as he rose and stepped out into the hallway.

A nurse was walking towards him.

"Excuse me, nurse," Arwyn said as he stopped her and read her name badge, "Nurse Smith,"

"You can call me Bryony, constable," the nurse smiled at him.

"Thank you, Bryony. Could you please sit with her ladyship whilst I find her doctor, please? I don't think she should be left alone," Arwyn asked.

"Of course," the nurse smiled, and the constable thanked her before he set off in search of the records room.

It took him longer to find than he would have liked, but the room was locked, and there was no answer from inside.

The clerk must have gone home for the day, he thought to himself and sighed. He kept searching, stopping every nurse and doctor he saw to ask about Doctor Hales' whereabouts, but no one had seen him recently.

He began to worry that Lady Sarah's suspicions were not groundless and the doctor might be in grave danger. He was musing on what to do next and where the doctor could be when a familiar voice called out to him.

"Why Constable Evans! What a pleasant surprise. What brings you to the hospital at this hour?" Edward Egerton called out in a friendly voice.

Arwyn looked up to see Thomas and Edward Egerton walking down the corridor with Charlotte Egerton and Mary Pierrepont.

"Mr Egerton, Mr Egerton, Mrs Egerton, Miss Pierrepont," Arwyn said formerly as he nodded his head to each of them in turn.

"You look worried, constable, what is wrong?" Charlotte asked with concern.

"It is nothing I should worry you with, though I assume you have all come to visit Lady Sarah," Constable Evans replied.

"We have indeed," Thomas said brightly, "We thought she could use some merry company of an evening."

"Good, good. Would you be kind enough to stay with her until I return? I must go fetch some help," Arwyn requested with a solemn look on his face.

"Of course, but constable, please confide in us. What is wrong?" Mary said, her eyes wide with alarm.

"Lady Sarah will tell you all you wish to know, I am sure. I am sorry, but I must go. I fear I have not a moment to lose," the constable said and dashed off leaving the company of four looking after him with a mixture of surprise and dismay.

Chapter 14

Doctor Hales' head ached as he opened his eyes.

His vision was blurred, and it took a moment for his eyes to adjust to his surroundings. He was in a very small room. The walls were damp but showed signs of wealth that would have been evident if the room had been maintained properly.

There was no furniture in the room, but Jack Hales was not alone, either. A man was lying on the floor a few feet away from him.

"You're finally awake then," the man croaked as he looked over at the doctor.

"Yes, I don't suppose you know where we are?" Doctor Hales asked as he tried to stand up, but found his legs were too weak to support his own weight, and he was soon back on the floor.

"No clue, I'm afraid," the man coughed.

"Are you alright?" Jack asked with concern as he crawled over to examine the man.

"No, I don't believe so, but there is nothing that can

be done from in here. I'm Marcus, Doctor Marcus Duckett," the man said as he gasped for breath.

"Doctor Jack Hales, a pleasure," Jack said dryly as he tried to help Marcus to sit up.

"What brings you here?" Marcus asked.

"I was looking for you," Jack said and laughed to himself a little before he continued, "My apologies. A good friend asked me to investigate some supposed disappearances. It led me to paperwork with your name on it that was a disgrace and left me with many questions about the patients that were named in the documents. I couldn't find you at the hospital, but a nurse told me that she would bring me to you. It seems she kept her word, though not quite how I expected she would," Doctor Hales explained.

"Well, at the very least you have found me. I don't suppose the nurse left the paperwork with you?" Doctor Duckett asked.

"No, I fear she left me with only my clothes," Jack replied with annoyance.

"I thought not. Though the paperwork has my name upon it, it is not I that is responsible for filling out the papers or filing them. That is the domain of my nurse, Bryony Smith.

She is the one that deals with that on my behalf," Marcus sighed and fought the urge to cough again.

"She is the very nurse that said she would bring me to you. How did you come to be here?" Doctor Hales asked as he moved to lean back against the wall.

"I noticed that some of the patients at the hospital were disappearing. To begin with, it was one or two a month. But as time has gone on, more and more patients have disappeared. I tried to find their paperwork to see if I could find out what was happening. The next thing I knew, I was in this room. It feels like I have been here for an eternity, but it cannot have been more than a few days. At least I hope that it has not been more than a few days," Marcus rasped and clutched at his chest for a moment.

"I see, then we are both here for the same reason, and it would seem that Nurse Smith is involved in it all somehow. I would hate to think what is happening to these poor patients that are vanishing, but I am more concerned about your health. It is far too damp in here for you with that chest," Doctor Hales said with his most concerned doctor's expression.

"Unfortunately, I do not think we are able to change

rooms in this establishment," Marcus chuckled to himself and regretted the mirth as it sparked a second coughing fit.

"Perhaps not, but my friend will alert the authorities and not allow them to rest until we have been found. For the moment we should sit by the window and try to get you as much fresh air as we can," Doctor Hales said as he glanced over at the boarded-up windows and hoped that the windows beyond the boards have a few panes missing.

Chapter 15

Thomas, Edward, Charlotte and Mary did not wait in the hallway for long. The moment Arwyn had disappeared from sight, and they had all recovered from the initial shock of what was happening around them, they hurried through the hospital to Lady Sarah's room.

Not only were they keen to see how she fared, but they also knew that she could answer the burning questions that each of them had about what was going on in the hospital.

The door to Lady Sarah's room was open, and as the four companions piled into the room, they found that it was empty. Lady Sarah's bed was lying on its side, and the blankets, sheets and pillows were strewn across the floor.

"What on earth is happening in this place?" Thomas asked with wide eyes as he took in the scene.

"I don't know, but we should see if we can find out where Lady Sarah has gone. Charlotte, Mary, you are to stay here, close the door and put something against it. Don't open it until either we come back or Constable Evans returns," Edward said firmly.

Charlotte and Mary looked at each other anxiously but nodded their agreement.

Thomas and Edward promised to be careful as they left Lady Sarah's room and shut the door behind them. They could hear the sound of the bed being wheeled across the floor and were satisfied that Charlotte and Mary were safe enough for the moment.

"Where do you think we should start?" Edward asked as he looked up and down the corridor.

"We need to ask if anyone saw her or heard anything. There are plenty of staff in this place, someone must have seen or heard something," Thomas replied.

"Do we each pick a direction and meet back here, or should we go together?" Edward asked, feeling uneasy about walking around the hospital alone.

"You don't think it is safe to go alone?" Thomas frowned at his brother.

"Lady Sarah is missing from her room, Constable Evans has gone to fetch more officers of the law, whatever is happening here I would rather not meet it alone," Edward shrugged. Thomas smiled at his brother and shook his head.

"What would Captain Wilbraham Egerton think of his brave little brothers?" Thomas chuckled to himself.

"I would be very glad if he were here right now instead of in India," Edward sighed and began to walk down the hall.

"So would mother. Charles and Charlotte are coming back to Tatton Park for Christmas, no doubt with Margaret in tow. She has not said as much, but I think she would be happier if we were all together for the festive season. Father will be bringing them back when Parliament closes, and from what I heard this morning, they may have another guest with them," Thomas replied as he fell into step beside his brother.

"Well, then we will have to prepare for all the eligible men in the kingdom descending upon the house. Wilbraham would certainly have enjoyed playing the protective older brother with military rank." Edward laughed in spite of the situation.

"I am sure he would have done more than rattle his sabre to scare off the more undeserving rascals that tipped their hat in Lottie's direction," Thomas grinned.

The topic of family was something that both Thomas

and Edward had always found calming. On the outside, there seemed to be nothing wrong as the two men walked down the corridor, jovially discussing their siblings and parents.

But underneath their composed façades, both men were terrified. They were worried about the safety of their missing friend, they were worried about the safety of their lady loves, and they were worried about their own safety.

Yet, they were both men that had been raised by a proud father and two older brothers that valued chivalry above all else. When a friend was in danger, or a woman was in distress, then it was their duty to help, no matter the risk to themselves.

In this case, Lady Sarah appeared to be a friend in danger and a woman in distress. Though the police would arrive shortly, both Thomas and Edward would have been ashamed if they had cowered in the hospital room instead of looking for the missing lady.

Every nurse or doctor that the paid came across was stopped and questioned. None of them had seen any sign of Lady Sarah or heard anything that would make them think that Lady Sarah had been taken against her will.

Not only did they ask the medical staff, but they also asked the patients that were able to speak with them. By the time they had made their way back to Lady Sarah's room, they were none the wiser to where she had gone.

"Do you think she left of her own accord?" Edward asked his brother as they leant against the wall outside the hospital room.

Neither man wanted to go back to the room without having something close to good news to report to Charlotte and Mary.

"No. She's been so ill recently she wouldn't have the strength to stand, let alone sneak out of the hospital without being seen by anyone. Besides, why would she overturn the bed?" Thomas said as he shook his head.

"Then what do we tell the ladies?" Edward sighed.

"The truth. It may not be a happy truth, but we shouldn't linger here. There are cabs outside the hospital, we can send Charlotte and Mary home then wait for Constable Evans. He needs to know that Lady Sarah is missing and do whatever we can to help find her," Thomas replied firmly.

"Very well. The sooner Mary and Charlotte are away from this place, the happier I shall be," Edward said as he moved to knock on the door to the hospital room.

"You are not the only one," Thomas agreed.

Chapter 16

Charlotte and Mary were escorted hurriedly through the hospital. The two women were scared and close to tears as they reached the entrance and the cold night air on their faces was a welcome relief to them both.

The chill of winter in the air was a safety blanket wrapping around them, pulling them away from the danger that the hospital offered.

The moment that the two women had set foot outside, both Thomas and Edward felt a weight lift from their shoulders. They were still anxious about the whereabouts of Lady Sarah, but their first concern would always be Charlotte and Mary.

As they walked down the steps to the curb where a handsome cab was waiting, Mary stopped and looked back at the building.

"Please, be careful," she whispered to Edward as she tightly squeezed his arm.

"Don't worry, I will be," Edward whispered back.

There were three handsome cabs waiting in a line outside the hospital, opposite the park. The train station was not far from the hospital, and the park was quiet at this time of night that made it a good place for the cab drivers to rest their horses after a hard day.

Though they were resting the horses, they would still take passengers, especially nurses that were tired after a hard day's work and keen to get safely home to their families.

Charlotte climbed into the cab first and Marry clambered in behind her.

"Tatton Park, please," Thomas told the driver and pressed some coins into his hand.

"Very good, sir," the driver said, and the cab soon rolled off down the road.

"At least they are safe now," Edward sighed as he stared after the cab as it turned the corner and disappeared from view.

"Constable Evans will be back soon. Then we can tell him about Lady Sarah. I can't believe that she has completely disappeared though," Thomas shook his head with frustration.

"It seems impossible that a woman could vanish from

her hospital room without a soul seeing her," Edward agreed.

"'scuse me, sirs, you say someone has disappeared?" one of the cab drivers called down to the two men.

"Yes, why do you ask?" Thomas frowned at the cab driver.

"Well, sirs, I don't know when the lady you are speaking of disappeared, but an ambulance came out of the yard at a right pace a few hours ago. Just after a policeman left the hospital, I seem to remember," the cab driver said as he rubbed his chin.

"A policeman? Which direction did the ambulance go?" Edward asked with a frantic edge to his voice.

"That way," the man pointed down the street in the opposite direction to the one that the cab with Mary and Charlotte had taken.

"Who was driving it?" Thomas asked.

"A slight man, wrapped in a long dark coat and his hat was pulled all the way down so I couldn't see his face," the cab driver said as he scratched his head.

"Thank you," Edward said and gave the man a few coins.

"You're most welcome, sirs," the cab driver tipped his hat in thanks to the two men.

"Will you be here long?" Thomas asked.

"Per'aps an hour, sir," the cab driver replied.

"Good, there is a police constable who may want to speak to you," Thomas said and looked around to see if Arwyn had arrived with the other constables.

Thomas and Edward waited with the cab driver for half an hour before Arwyn finally came back.

"Mr Egerton, Mr Egerton, I thought you were waiting with Lady Sarah," Constable Evans greeted the two men of Tatton Park.

"Constable Evans, we were planning to, but unfortunately Lady Sarah wasn't in her room," Thomas replied coldly.

"What do you mean, sir?" Arwyn frowned.

Edward and Thomas glanced at one another. Thomas nodded at Edward, and Edward began to explain what they had found in the room and everything after.

The cab driver had his moment to explain about the ambulance, and when the story was finished, Arwyn sighed and looked thoughtfully between the three men.

"Constable Meyers, please accompany Mr Egerton and Mr Egerton back to Tatton Park," Arwyn said finally, "Just in case you remember anything else, sirs," the constable smiled.

Constable Meyers nodded and motioned for Edward and Thomas to lead the way. Arwyn watched as the two Mr Egertons made their way towards the yard at the back of the hospital where their carriage was waiting for them.

Constable McIntyre, Constables Clowes, and Constable Cantello had also accompanied Constable Evans to the hospital. There were few constables that Arwyn trusted after everything that he had seen happened since Lady Sarah had arrived in Stickleback Hollow, but the men he had called upon he not only knew were good officers, but men he counted amongst his friends too.

"What is your plan?" Constable McIntyre asked as Constable Evans left the cab driver and walked back over to the police wagons.

"If Lady Sarah has gone missing and she was taken away in the ambulance that the cab driver described, then she could be anywhere," Arwyn shrugged and screwed up his face as he thought. There was something niggling at the back of his mind that he couldn't remember, but he knew it was important.

"Are you sure she isn't somewhere in the hospital, along with the doctor?" Constable Cantello asked as he looked up at the hospital building. It was a towering structure that the constable imagine extended below ground, making it a building that was not easy for two men to search on their own in such a short space of time.

"I brought you to help me search the hospital because I believed the doctor had to be somewhere inside it. Whether he is trapped in a storage cupboard or in a locked room that has fallen into disuse, I don't know," Arwyn replied.

"Then we should search the hospital. Perhaps you would be best served looking for clues in the yard. If anyone was taken out to an ambulance there, they may have left something behind," Constable Clowes suggested.

"You're right. We should meet back here in an hour to discuss anything that we have found. If we find something that needs urgent attention, send a nurse or doctor to fetch the rest of us to you," Constable Evans said firmly, and the other three policemen nodded before making their way across the road to the hospital door.

Arwyn stood for a moment, trying to scour his mind for the thought that alluded him, but it was no good.

Perhaps if I go into the yard and stop trying to remember, it will come to me. Arwyn thought. His mother had always been a great believer in such a thing.

"The more you try to think about things like that, the more the thought will run from you. It's no good chasing stray thoughts around your head, they know the twists and turns of your mind better than you do. No, you are much better letting the thought run away and doing something else for a while. You'll find that thought comes running back to you on its own," Arwyn could remember her telling him this time and time again when he was a boy.

He sighed and decided that his mother knew best and that standing in the street all night was not likely to get him very far.

He checked the road for traffic before he crossed. Though there was always noise in the city, you could never quite be certain if it was the noise of something coming to knock you down without stopping to check.

He stopped at the entrance to the yard to let the carriage bound for Tatton Park pass him and noticed that there was a set of wheel prints in the mud that were deeper and wider than most carriages.

He followed the tracks into the yard and found they stopped next to the back door of the hospital. It was the door that deliveries were made through, and linens were taken away to be cleaned through.

Arwyn looked around for anything else. At the base of the door to the back of the hospital, there were flecks of mud on the steps, but there was no way to know how long they had been there or who had left then. The yard was covered with cobbles, and though there were patches of mud and the odd pile of horse manure, it was not a dirt yard that footprints could easily be found in. Aside from the tracks, there was nothing else in the yard to help Arwyn discover whether Lady Sarah had been taken from the hospital.

He sighed to himself and noticed that the doctor's trap was still in the yard. It hadn't even occurred to him that no one would have taken it back as Derwyn, Miss DeVille and the Egerton party had come in transport from the Grangeback and Tatton Park Estates.

He had his own police trap, but that could be returned by one of the other policemen to Stickleback

Hollow, and Arwyn could take them back to Chester that night, or they could sleep in the police house and be taken to the city in the morning.

He looked at the wheels on the doctor's trap and chuckled to himself. The doctor preferred large thin wheels on his transport. Wheels that were almost twice the size of normal carriage wheels. It was something that he and Henry Cartwright had shared. It was something that had become a running joke in Stickleback Hollow. If large wheels were trundling by it was either the doctor's cart or one of the carriages from Duffleton Hall.

He was about to head into the hospital to see how the search was going when the thought ran into him - Duffleton Hall.

It had been bought recently by a doctor and would be the perfect place for someone to take an ambulance in the night, especially if they didn't want others to find out who was in it.

Constable Evans rushed into the hospital and found a nurse who could pass on the message to the other constables about where he was going. He left the police wagon for the others in case they needed it and ran back to the yard to take the doctor's trap back to Stickleback Hollow, and from there he could go to Duffleton Hall.

Chapter 17

Thomas and Edward, though amiable for the most part, were not used to being given orders, especially by those of the working class. Neither felt particularly happy about returning to Tatton Park and when Arwyn went past them on the road out of the city at a clip that bordered on dangerous, the pair took the opportunity to bully poor Constable Meyers into following him.

Constable Evans was not in the police wagon, but the doctor's trap, and for him to take it and be driving it so fast told the Egerton boys that he had discovered something important.

Constable Meyers was quite adept at driving the carriage quickly, and though it was a little bumpy in the back for the Egerton boys, there was never a moment when the carriage seemed about to tip over.

The policeman managed to keep Constable Evans in view and began to slow down as they entered Stickleback Hollow.

"Why has he come here at such a rate?" Thomas wondered aloud as he looked out of the carriage window.

"I suspect that he has come to collect Hunter. I expected to see him at the hospital, but I am sure he had a good reason for not being there," Edward replied as the carriage passed Wilson's Inn.

It didn't take long for the Egertons to discover that Edward was right in his supposition. Arwyn stopped on the road that lay close to the lodge, and Constable Meyers stopped the Egertons carriage behind it.

"What are you doing here?" Arwyn demanded of Constable Meyers.

"We made him bring us," Thomas explained.

"Hunter!" Edward yelled as he moved past where Arwyn stood and walked into the trees towards the lodge, "HUNTER!"

Thomas ran after his brother, acting as an echo.

"Hunter!"

"Hunter!"

Arwyn rolled his eyes and sighed and followed after the pair. Constable Meyers stayed with the two carriages for the men to come back.

Edward and Thomas had reached the front door of the lodge before Arwyn caught up to them.

"Hunter, come out!" they cried as they hammered on the door.

"Go away!" Alex shouted back, his voice barely audible over the noise that the Egerton boys were making.

"No!" they shouted back.

"Hunter, Lady Sarah has vanished from the hospital," Arwyn called out as the Egerton boys paused for breath.

The door swung open suddenly, and Mr Hunter stood in the doorway, looking haggard and unkempt. The smell from inside the lodge was overpowering, so much so, Thomas and Edward had to back away from the door.

"She's missing?" he croaked.

"Yes, but I think I know where to find her. Doctor Hales is also missing," Constable Evans replied.

"You know where she went?" Edward asked with surprise.

"I think she may be at Duffleton Hall. A doctor I met once at the hospital bought Duffleton Hall to turn it into a sanatorium. If they are trying to make people disappear, what better place to hide them?" Arwyn asked.

"Are you going to look?" Mr Hunter enquired.

"Yes, I want you to come with me too," Arwyn replied.

"Is it just me, or does Lady Sarah seem to get kidnapped a lot?" Thomas asked in a hushed voice to his brother as he waited for Mr Hunter to decide whether he was going to help them look for Lady Sarah or not.

"No, it's not just you. She does seem to find herself in trouble more than your average lady," Edward replied with a shrug.

"Life with her around is never boring," Thomas agreed with a grin.

"If you need my help to find her, then I will come with you," Mr Hunter said at last as he stepped out of the door for the first time in days and drank in the cold night air.

Chapter 18

Lady Sarah did not remember what had happened to her. One moment she had been in the hospital bed, anxiously awaiting news of Doctor Hales, and the next she was in a room that looked like it had once been richly furnished, but was now filled with shrieking women lying on mattresses on the floor.

Her head felt foggy and heavy. Her body ached as though she had been thrown around and against something heavy.

Lady Sarah gingerly tried to sit up and take stock of her surroundings. There were roughly twenty other women in the room. There could have been a few more or less, but with Sarah's head swimming, it was hard for her to count accurately.

Each of the women was dressed in filthy clothing that was torn and smelt worse than the hospital did. Lady Sarah searched for a clean piece of fabric to press against her face to help keep the smell from her nose., but she found none that smelt any better than the rest of the room.

Her own clothing was unchanged from when she had been in the hospital, though it was somewhat dirtier than it had been for reasons that Lady Sarah did not want to think about.

"You're awake then," the woman closest to Lady Sarah said, "I suppose there are a lot of questions that you have," she sighed.

Lady Sarah frowned slightly at the woman's attitude and familiarity but nodded.

"Welcome to purgatory, though we all know that from here we are going to be in hell soon enough. There's a nurse that brought us all here. We were in the hospital one moment and then woke up here the next. Those that have been here the longest are the ones that are over in that corner," the woman pointed at a group of three women that were huddled together in the far corner, rocking backwards and forwards, muttering to one another.

"Those that have been here the shortest time are the ones that are screaming, you'll probably join them after they take you away for the first time," the woman tutted.

"Why are they screaming?" Lady Sarah asked as she

found her voice.

"They still have hope. They think that screaming will somehow lead to their rescue, or that their screaming will make the nurse stop, but eventually, the screaming stops. And when it does, they become like me. The sooner you accept that you'll die here, the easier this will be for everyone," the woman said, shaking her head.

"Why would we die here?" Lady Sarah asked with no small amount of fear in her voice.

"The nurse, she has a vendetta against women like us. She is experimenting on us, causing pain and slowly draining our lives away. She drugs us, leaves us here to live in our own filth with scars and open wounds. She barely feeds us and the water left for us is stale and fetid," the woman sneered.

"What kind of experiments is she doing?" Lady Sarah asked as she tried to get to her feet. Her legs gave way and fell back down on her first attempt, but it did not stop the young woman from trying to get up again. Eventually, she managed to get to her feet, but she had to lean on the wall for support.

"Do I look like a nurse or a doctor? I don't know what

the experiments are or even what they are for. I only know that it's painful. No, not just painful, it is pain beyond belief, pain that reaches deep into your soul and threatens to rip your soul out of your body. You can't help but beg for her to stop her torturous endeavours, but your pleas fall on deaf ears. She keeps on doing as she pleases until the pain is so great that you pass out." the woman replied.

"What did you mean by 'women like us'?" Lady Sarah asked, "You don't know my name, I don't know yours, how could you know we have anything in common?"

"Every woman in this room was pregnant. Every woman in this room is unmarried. You are in this room, so you must be unmarried and have been pregnant," the woman said wearily, looking at Lady Sarah with an empty expression. There was no judgement, no condescension, just a statement of fact.

"All of you?" Lady Sarah asked with wide eyes.

"And you," the woman said flatly.

"What is your name?" Lady Sarah asked the woman as she tried to take a few steps.

"Does it matter? Having a name is a place like this is pointless. We won't get to leave, sharing our memories and our lives before this place only gives you something to miss and long for. It hurts your heart too much. You'd be best to out any thoughts of your life out of your head. It won't help you here," the woman said as she stood up and walked off.

Lady Sarah watched her walk across to the other side of the room and sit down on one of the mattresses. Sarah thought the woman's behaviour was odd, but as she looked around the room, she saw that there were three distinct groups of women in the room. The ones that were huddled together in the corner of the room, rocking back and forth, muttering to themselves. The ones that were holding onto one another, screaming and crying, and finally, the ones that were sat on mattresses with a cold, dead look in their eyes.

The last group didn't talk to each other, they didn't do anything, they just sat there and didn't move. Every so often, they would cast dirty looks at the screaming women, but they never shouted at them or did anything to try and quieten them.

She took a deep breath and realised that the smell was not so bad away from the mattress and the other women. The stench seemed to be confined to fabrics and skin rather than having seeped into the building itself. There was another smell under it all, something familiar to Lady Sarah, like the rooms of Grangeback that were left shut up for too long.

"How long have you been here?" Lady Sarah asked in a raised voice. She wasn't asking anyone in particular, but a few of the women looked up at her. The screaming women didn't stop, nor did they cast their eyes in her direction.

"How could we know?" the woman that had been speaking to her asked, "We have no way to tell time, no way to know what day it is, let alone the date."

"You can't have been here that long," Lady Sarah replied.

"And what makes you say that?" the woman asked snidely.

"Because there is the smell of dust and dry rot underneath all the filth. That only comes when a place has been empty for a long time," Lady Sarah replied and managed to stagger a few steps towards where the woman sat.

"We haven't been here that long. A few days at most. Before we were in a room in the hospital. At least it smelt like the hospital, and the walls looked the same," another one offered helpfully.

"So you were brought here recently?" Lady Sarah asked and closed her eyes to think for a moment. There seemed to be one thing that all the women in the room had in common, fear. It was shown in different ways, but all of the women were afraid.

If they had been kept in the hospital somewhere, they would have to be kept locked up and as far from other patients as possible to avoid being discovered. This place seemed more like a country home than a hospital, and as Lady Sarah knew from Grangeback, not all of the doors would lock.

Fear and the thought that they had been locked in before would keep the women from trying the door. Not knowing what this nurse was doing to the women, or would do if she caught Lady Sarah meant that she did not share the fear that held these women captive.

As far as Lady Sarah could see, there were two things that she could do. Firstly, she could sit and wait to see what would happen. She knew that when Arwyn found her gone, he would come looking for her, but as she didn't know where she was, it would be unlikely that he would be able to find her quickly. Secondly, she could look around this place and see if she could find any way to escape.

The second course of action was the only sensible one to take as far as Lady Sarah was concerned, there were risks with both courses of action, but trying to escape rather than just waiting to be rescued was far more palatable to the young lady.

She didn't say anything to the other women as she made her way across the room. Her legs were slowly beginning to respond, and each step she took, they moved more easily. They stopped threatening to collapse, much to Lady Sarah's relief and got her safely to the door.

She took a deep breath, unaware that most of the women in the room were staring at her in disbelief, and put her hand on the door handle. She turned it slowly and felt the door opening towards her.

"Don't," the first woman said with terror in her voice.

"I have to. If I find a way out, I will come back for you," Lady Sarah said softly, without turning around.

Chapter 19

Lady Sarah opened the door wide enough so that she could see out into the corridor beyond. There was nobody there, and no sounds of footsteps could be heard.

Lady Sarah slipped out through the door and closed it quietly behind her.

The hallway was dim and covered with dust. It was clear that it had been months since anyone had cleaned the house properly. The smell of dry rot and dust was much stronger now that she was in the hallway.

The corridor stretched on either side of Lady Sarah, and there was no clear way to go.

Left or Right? she thought, *Left.*

She put her hand out to use the wall to help her walk and also to help keep her from getting lost in the dim light. Each time her hand felt a door, she tried the handle and looked into the room to see what was in there.

Four rooms after the one she had escaped from and all Lady Sarah had found was piles of broken furniture and even more dust.

There was a turn in the corridor ahead, and boarded windows lined the wall. All of the boards were securely in place, and those that did not have boards on the inside were firmly shuttered from the outside.

At the end of the corridor was a door that when she opened it, Lady Sarah found led to the kitchen. The kitchen had some provisions in it and clean water. She was tempted to stop and try to wash herself down, but as much as she hated being dirty, it could wait until after she had found a way out of the house.

She made her way carefully around the kitchen until she reached the backdoor and tried it. It opened. Her heart leapt inside her chest. She closed the door, resisting the urge to rush out of it to go for help.

Lady Sarah had no way of knowing where she was or how long it would be before she could find help. Going back to fetch the other women and escaping together was better than leaving them behind. If they were moved again before Lady Sarah came back with help, there would be no way to know where they were taken.

Something else gnawed at Lady Sarah's mind too.

There were enough women in that room to overpower a single nurse. It was only the nurse that the woman had mentioned to Lady Sarah. Still, there had to be other people involved, more of them in order to keep the women quiet, to move them unseen through the hospital, to have the medical knowledge to perform experiments.

Yet, there was no one that Lady Sarah had seen and no sign of anyone else in the house. There had to be wardsmen and a doctor involved at the very least.

As Lady Sarah was pondering this, the sound of voices filtered into the kitchen through a vent in the wall. She couldn't tell what they were saying, but they must have been nearby to carry through the vent.

Lady Sarah cautiously made her way back through the kitchen and looked for a door that led off in the same direction that the voices were coming from.

There was a door that led from the kitchen into another dark passageway. She listened carefully, trying to see if the sound of voices was coming from somewhere down the corridor, but she couldn't make out anything.

She snuck as deftly as she could down the corridor, stopping to press her ear against each door to listen for voices.

After she tried listening at three doors, she finally found the one she had been looking for, but rather than try to listen at the door, or even enter the room, she backtracked to one of the rooms that she thought was empty and slipped inside.

There was nothing different about this room to any of the other rooms that she had seen in the house. It was dusty, void of furniture, but there was a vent in the skirting board that Sarah could hear what was being said in the next room through.

"How long do you expect to keep us here?" a well-known voice demanded. It belonged to Doctor Hales. Sarah felt relief wash over her that the doctor was safe.

"As long as I want to. No one will find you here," a woman replied. The voice seemed familiar to Lady Sarah as well, but she couldn't quite place it.

One of the nurses from the hospital? She wondered to herself.

"People will be looking for both of us," Jack Hales replied with a slight growl.

"They can look all they like, they will never find you

here. Come, Bertie, Alfred, we have to prepare for the procedure for our new arrival," the nurse said.

Looking through the vent, Lady Sarah could see three pairs of shoes through the vent, one of them clearly belonged to the nurse, the others must have belonged the Bertie and Alfred that she mentioned.

She watched as the three of them turned and walked out of her line of sight. The door to the room opened and closed, and the sound of footsteps could be heard disappearing down the corridor.

Lady Sarah waited for the footsteps to fade before she opened the door to the room she was in and rushed to enter the room with the doctor in.

She shut the door hurriedly and was surprised to see another man was in the room with Doctor Hales. Neither of the men were tied up in the cold and damp room, and Sarah wondered how the two men were being kept there.

"Lady Sarah!" Doctor Hales said with surprise, "What are you doing here?"

"I was taken from my hospital room and woke up here. Who is this?" Lady Sarah asked.

"Doctor Marcus Duckett, the man that was the doctor

for the disappearing patients but it seems one of the nurses and a few wardsmen are behind the disappearances," Jack replied.

"I don't know exactly what has been going on here, but I know we need to leave. I found a way out, but I need to go back for the other women being held here," Lady Sarah replied.

"How many women are there?" Doctor Duckett asked.

"Around twenty, some have lost their minds, but the rest are just scared of what is going to happen to them," Lady Sarah said hurriedly.

"Then you should go and get the women out of here. Come back for us when they are safe, and you have been able to fetch Constable Evans," Doctor Hales sighed.

"Why won't you come with us?" Lady Sarah asked.

"That nurse, she keeps us drugged so we can't leave. I don't know what exactly she is using, but it robs me of all my strength. I can't stand, it's a challenge to breathe half the time," Jack said as he rasped for air.

"I can't leave you here," Lady Sarah said firmly.

"You must. At least for now. Get the women to safety,

then you can come back for us. Please," Doctor Hales begged.

Lady Sarah nodded slowly and quickly left the room. She stopped in the hallway and took a deep breath to keep herself from crying. She knew that the doctor was right and that saving twenty women from torture was better than rescuing one friend that was being drugged to keep him as a prisoner, but it didn't make her feel any better about abandoning a man that had been so kind and understanding during one of the worst times of her life.

Lady Sarah did not tarry long in the hallway. Instead, she moved quickly back to the kitchen and then back to the room the women were held in.

"There's a way out, but we have to go now," Lady Sarah announced and their screaming finally stopped.

Chapter 20

The Egertons carriage and the doctor's trap pulled up outside Duffleton Hall in the same moment that the police wagon arrived.

"I see you got my message," Arwyn said as he climbed down and greeted Constable Clowes.

"We couldn't find anything at the hospital, so though this might be a better use of our time," Constable Cantello replied as he leapt down from the other side of the cart. Constable McIntyre stepped out of the back of the wagon as Constable Clowes opened the back door for him.

"We should go in and look around," Mr Hunter growled; his lack of patience due in part to his pounding head as much as concern for Lady Sarah's safety.

"No, we need to look around the outside first. See if we can't find any signs of life in there first, then we go in," Constable McIntyre said firmly.

"He's right, Alex, we should split up into two groups, and one group will go around the right side of the house, and the other group -" Constable Evans began.

"Will look after this large group of women that are running towards us being led by Lady Sarah?" Thomas asked with a grin on his face. The men spun around to see close to thirty women staggering around the side of the house, crying and gasping as they moved.

All of them, including Lady Sarah, were dressed in soiled clothing and many looked gaunt and sickly.

"Your ladyship!" Arwyn called out with relief and rushed over, with Mr Hunter beside him.

Sarah smiled weakly before she collapsed to her knees, tears running down her face.

"Please, inside, Doctor Hales and another man are being held prisoner. They can't walk, you need to go get them," Lady Sarah begged Mr Hunter, who nodded and ran towards the house with Constables Clowes and McIntyre not far behind.

"What has been happening here?" Arwyn asked.

"I don't know the full extent of the horrors they have been through, but I know that a nurse and two wardsmen are in charge here. I suspect that there is more to it, but -" Lady Sarah's voice trailed off as she looked back at the building and realised where she was, "Duffleton?"

"Mr Egerton, please can you help, I think Lady Sarah needs to be taken home," Arwyn said to Thomas.

"Not until I see Doctor Hales," Sarah said as Thomas tried to help her to her feet.

"Please, Wattie, you don't look well," Thomas said gently.

"Wattie?" Lady Sarah frowned with confusion.

"Charlotte and Mary thought you needed a nickname, can't very well go around calling you by that mouthful of a title all the time, and Sarah is a little too formal for our little sister, Lottie, so we thought Wattie was a good fit," Thomas explained.

"I've never had a nickname before," Lady Sarah smiled.

She allowed Thomas to lift her to her feet and help her towards the Egertons' carriage. Edward and Arwyn took care of the women that had come out of Duffleton Hall with Sarah, whilst Constables Meyers and Cantello went to search the house for those responsible.

It was almost half an hour before Alex emerged from the house carrying Doctor Hales in his arms, Constables

McIntyre and Clowes behind them with Doctor Duckett.

The women were scared but allowed themselves to be loaded into the police wagon, but there were so many of them, Constable Evans, Clowes and McIntyre had to take the doctor's trap to Grangeback to fetch the two large hay wagons, with Lady Sarah's permission.

It seemed to take half the night to load all of the women into the wagons, but by the time they had all found a place to sit, Constables Meyers and Cantello returned to report that the house was empty. They had found some terrible things inside the house, but those responsible had vanished.

"What a shame that Pattinson isn't here, he would have been able to sniff them out in an instant," Edward said to Mr Hunter, causing the groundskeeper to scowl at his friend and stalk off to wait with Doctor Hales.

Doctor Duckett was put in one of the hay wagons with the women and all the policeman, save for Arwyn, departed for Chester. Arwyn would follow after he had put the doctor to bed and returned Mr Hunter to the lodge.

Lady Sarah was entrusted to Edward and Thomas' care, knowing the Egerton boys would make sure she got home safely.

There were a lot of questions to ask the women, but for the moment they were grateful to be out of the squalid room they had been held in.

"Take good care of them," Lady Sarah urged the constables as the wagons rolled by.

"Hey, your ladyship, you wanted to know my name? It's Silvia," the woman that had been so cool and cold was now smiling, and her face shone brightly under the soft moonlight.

"Thank you," Lady Sarah smiled back.

"Come on, Ted, time this lady was home in bed," Thomas said as he climbed up beside his brother and the two turned their carriage away from Duffleton Hall for a much better prospect - Grangeback.

Chapter 21

Mrs Bosworth, Cooky and Bosworth were all waiting outside the manor house along with Derwyn when the Egertons carriage pulled up.

There was so much joy at Lady Sarah's return that no one questioned her condition. Mrs Bosworth took her straight off to have a hot bath and be put to bed.

Thomas and Edward were shown to two of the guest rooms for the night, and there was no arguing with Mrs Bosworth when she decided that there were to be guests.

Cooky set to work cooking something good for Lady Sarah to eat and left her some sweet plum cakes on the table in her bedroom to eat when she woke up.

In the morning, Stanley and Lee Baker were so shocked to find Lady Sarah was home, they refused to leave her side, and Pattinson was there to greet her as well. Miss DeVille had taken charge of the dog when Arwyn had been called to visit Lady Sarah and brought him up to Grangeback where she knew he would be well looked after.

Only one person was missing from the happy scene at breakfast that morning who wasn't on the other side of the world.

Mr Hunter had spent a sleepless night at the lodge and come to a final decision. When morning had come, he had sat down and written a letter, waiting until he knew that Bosworth would be up to deliver it to the main house.

When the rest of the household had finished their breakfast and left the table, Bosworth brought the letter to Lady Sarah.

She decided that outside was the best place to read, even though it was cold, the day was bright, and she had been inside for far too long.

Pattinson happily followed her outside, and the pair made their way to the bench in the rose garden that Lady Sarah liked to sit on when she wanted privacy.

She slowly opened the letter and began to read:

Sarah,

When we first met, I was convinced that you were like every other rich person that I have been around in my life.

When I discovered you weren't, I couldn't help but fall in love with you. Despite our different stations in life, I found you loved me too. There was so much I was looking forward to in our lives together when my father told me of heritage and how he would recognise me as his son, but with his departure, your pregnancy and now the miscarriage, I have realised that should we continue on our path together, it will only lead to your ruin. I cannot marry you and drag your name and reputation into disrepute. I cannot stay in Stickleback Hollow either.

By the time you read this letter, I will be gone. I do not know if I will return, but wherever I go in the world, know that I will think the best of you, even though I know that you will think the worst of me.

Alex

Tears fell from Lady Sarah's eyes and splattered all over the letter, causing the ink to run. She screwed up the letter and cried bitterly. Pattinson lay his head in her lap and whined, offering her some small measure of comfort. Lady Sarah dropped to her knees and threw her arms around the neck of the dog as she cried, burying her face in his fur.

She cried for a few minutes until she could cry no more. She let go of Pattinson, wiped her eyes on a handkerchief and composed herself. Though she was heartbroken, it was her pain to bear and no one else's. She crushed the letter in the palm of her hand and walked slowly back to the house, Pattinson walking behind her.

When she reached the kitchen, she opened the door of the oven and threw the letter inside. The fire wasn't lit, but the letter would burn soon enough.

She made her way into the drawing room and sat quietly with her hands folded as she stared out of the window.

Every fibre of her being wanted to go to the stables, saddle Black Guy and ride screaming all over the estate, but she knew she was not strong enough to ride just yet and that sitting alone for a moment would be better for her sanity.

Mrs Bosworth knew that the letter from Alex had arrived at the house, and that Lady Sarah had gone into the garden to read the letter. She waited in the hallway for Lady Sarah to come back in. When Mrs Bosworth saw Sarah throw the letter into the oven, she waited until her ladyship was in the drawing room before she retrieved the letter.

She read it twice before she threw it back into the oven, knowing that it was a letter that was best left to be burnt.

Mrs Bosworth felt so disappointed in Mr Hunter and was certain that when the brigadier came home, he would be as heartbroken by his son's behaviour as Lady Sarah must be.

Derwyn had gone out almost as soon as he had finished breakfast and was not expected back until later that night, so it surprised Lady Sarah when she saw Derwyn and Miss DeVille accompanied by Mr Claydon Mitchell and Miss Beaumont arriving at the house.

Bosworth announced them in the drawing room. Mrs Bosworth brought tea, and it was clear that the joy of Lady Sarah's return to Grangeback extended to the people of Stickleback Hollow too.

The company stayed through lunch, and it was mid-afternoon before they made ready to leave, but as they were departing, Miss Beaumont and Miss DeVille paused and smiled at Lady Sarah, clearly wanting to say something but not sure how to share their news.

"What is it?" Lady Sarah asked as she looked between

the two couples.

"Well, your ladyship, Derwyn and myself, we finally asked these two delightful ladies to marry us," Claydon said with a beaming smile upon his face.

"How wonderful, congratulations!" Lady Sarah said with warmth and genuine affection for the pair.

"We'll be getting married here in Stickleback Hollow," Miss Beaumont explained.

"And we'll be getting married back in Wales," Miss DeVille said with excitement.

"But we are both agreed that we couldn't get married without you there, please say you'll come," Derwyn pleaded.

"Of course, I will be delighted to be there," Lady Sarah replied. They said their goodbyes at the door, and Lady Sarah felt the desire to cry again.

"Your ladyship, I know that it won't help much, but I am so very proud of you," Mrs Bosworth said as she appeared in the hallway.

"Can you tell Bosworth that I cannot see any more visitors today? I need some time to myself," Lady Sarah replied in a quiet voice.

"I shall do, my lady," Mrs Bosworth agreed.

"Thank you, I will be in the garden," the young lady said and made her way out to walk the grounds so that she could deal with her pain without anyone to see it. She knew that Mrs Bosworth meant well, but it was still an invasion of her privacy, and there were some things that Lady Sarah wanted to keep just to herself.

Pattinson followed her as she stepped outside and pulled her cloak close about her shoulders. She was a few steps down the path when she saw a man walking towards the house. He was tall, not quite as tall as Mr Hunter, but still tall and well dressed.

He was not known to Lady Sarah, but she stopped and waited to see how Pattinson reacted to him. The dog began to bark and ran towards the man. The man stopped and knelt down to greet the dog.

Pattinson leapt around joyfully and barked as the man stroked him, then the dog rushed back to Lady Sarah's side, the man following him.

"Good afternoon, ma'am, I am sorry to be calling so late," the man spoke with a strange accent.

"Good afternoon, sir, what brings you to my door?" Lady Sarah asked with a wry smile. The man that was stood before her was handsome had kind eyes and was quick to smile.

He had dark brown eyes and sandy brown hair that was neatly brushed back and didn't appear to be disturbed by the top hat he wore.

"I came to introduce myself. My name is Oliver Henry Brown, ma'am. I am a cousin of the Egerton family of Tatton Park. I have come to settle in England from America," he replied with a bow, taking off his hat as he did so.

"Lady Sarah Montgomery Baird Watson-Wentworth, it's a pleasure to meet you," Sarah said, offering her hand to the gentleman. He gently took hold of her hand and kissed the back of it.

"My Lady, I look forward to making a closer acquaintance with you. My cousins tell me some very interesting stories about your exploits," Oliver smiled roguishly as he stood upright and replaced his hat.

"Would you like to accompany me on a turn about the garden? I would like to hear about America and what delights of England have brought you here," Lady Sarah offered.

"It would be my pleasure, my lady."

Chapter 22

Nurse Bryony Smith managed to escape the police along with her wardsmen. There were a few places to hide in Duffleton Hall that the police would never know to check which allowed them to stay hidden until the police had gone.

She couldn't go back to the hospital, so there was only one place that she knew she could go. The home of Doctor Marcus Duckett was empty when she arrived, so she let herself in and waited for the doctor to return.

It took several hours for the doctor to be brought home by the police, but when he arrived home, he was tired, and his patience was wearing thin.

"Are you here?" he asked grumpily when the door shut behind him.

"I am," Bryony replied.

"That was too close. You shouldn't have taken that Doctor Hales or Lady Sarah. But it's no matter. We can move on to a new city, under new names. It won't be very difficult to do. The information we gathered this time was very interesting, but my experiments are by no means complete," Doctor Duckett said.

"They don't suspect you at all?" Bryony asked.

"No, they believe that it was just you and the two wardsmen. Will you bring them?" Marcus inquired as he came into the living room and sat in one of the large chairs by the fire.

"No, they've gone out drinking. They'll meet with an unfortunate accident on their way home. There are always strong men in need of money who don't like police," Bryony shrugged.

"Our benefactor will be pleased, Fitzwilliam doesn't like loose ends, and everything we are doing is of great value to him. Which city do you want to go to?" Marcus asked with a wry smile.

"Leeds first, then perhaps London, there are so many places that we can go that people won't question the disappearance of a certain class of women," Bryony replied.

"Indeed, but this time, let's avoid taking anyone of importance," the doctor said dryly.

"Agreed."

~*~*~

Thanks for reading *The Advent of Stickleback Hollow!* Need to know what happens next?

She has one shot to pull off the perfect village Christmas party. But bloodstains under the mistletoe hide a sinister surprise.

Get *Christmas in Stickleback Hollow* now to see where Lady Sarah's next adventure leads.

~*~*~

Looking for more than just books? You can get the latest releases from C.S. Woolley, signed paperbacks and hardbacks, mugs, t-shirts, journals and much more from the all new Read Round the Clock Shopify store.

~*~*~

Love the Mysteries of Stickleback Hollow? Not caught up with the rest of the series, then jump back to A Thief in Stickleback Hollow, Book 1 in the Mysteries of Stickleback Hollow and see how it all began.

Want to help a reader out? Review are crucial when it comes to helping readers choose their next book and you can help them by leaving just a few sentences about this book as a review. It doesn't have to be anything fancy, just what you liked about the book and who you think might like to read it. **Scan the QR Code below** or visit

https://mybook.to/adventstickleback

If you don't have time to leave a review or don't feel confident writing one, recommending a book to your family, friends and co-workers can help them choose their next book, so feel free to spread the word.

Historical Note

The 5th November is a date that is still celebrated in the UK. It marks the foiled attempt of the Gunpowder Plot to blow up the Houses of Parliament in London. The most famous of the conspirators involved in the Gunpowder Plot was Guy Fawkes. An effigy of Fawkes is often burned on top of bonfires held to mark the occasion. Firework displays are also held.

Remember, Remember, the fifth of November, gunpowder, treason and plot. I see no reason, why gunpowder treason, should ever be forgot.

It is known a Bonfire Night in the United Kingdom and Fireworks Night in Canada, New Zealand and other countries. The night itself is not a celebration of a terrorist, as many social media keyboard warriors seem to believe, but is, in fact, a night where Guy Fawkes is ceremonially executed every year for his treason so that it is not forgotten and we celebrate the foiling of the plot.

Reputations and ruination were a genuine concern for most women within Victorian society. The concept of the Fallen Woman is not used much today, but simply put is a woman who is seen to be fallen from the grace of God. It mostly became associated with chastity and promiscuity. However, to begin with, it was associated with knowledge (connection to Eve taking the fruit from the Tree of Knowledge) but became more closely connected to sexual knowledge and experience. When a woman gained the reputation of being a fallen woman - whether from simply having a good education at one end of the scale or engaging in prostitution at the other end of the scale,

These women were outcast from society, and life was made extremely hard from them. There were projects created by moral and upright women to "rescue" fallen women, but fallen women were judged by these groups as to who was worth saving and those that weren't. Though we no longer use the term fallen woman in modern society, we still practise a similar form of judgement over who is worth giving help to when struggling and those who are undeserving of help.

The idea of an Englishman's home being his castle came into its own during the Victorian age, and because of this, Victorians were a little bit obsessed with their homes. Men, and some women, would leave the house every day in order to work rather than working in their homes every day. Working all day and returning home at the end of it to the warmth of their home was an important aspect of life. Fires were the most common way of heating a home, mostly powered by coal and wood, but there was also the development of radiant boiler-powered heat, and gas lighting.

Coal was not in short supply, and because of that was cheap. This meant that only the rich could afford the radiant heat of boilers, whereas the working and middle class maintained fires. A working class man would earn about 1 pound a week. Each pound (under the pounds, shilling and pence monetary system of the Victorian age) was worth 240 pence. A weeks supply of coal for a home cost about 1 shilling and 3 pence (23 pence).

The use of the coal fire was very dirty though, so there was often soot not only floating about the house, but soot would get onto the food and the fireplaces required daily cleaning.

Prior to the Victorian period, there were taverns and inns that offered food, drink and beds to travellers. But during the Victorian Age, there was the development of the Public House that were there to serve alcohol and mostly serve men, not women. Women that drank at these establishments were seen as poor mothers or fallen women.

Dram shops were places that sold alcohol, mostly spirits such as gin, direct to the public. They were often found in pharmacies and sold either a single shot of gin to drink then and there or bottles to be taken away by the customer. These Dram Shops began life in the 1700s and by the turn of the century, due to the cheap price of gin, had soaring numbers. But as beer and the Public House were introduced, Dram Shops began to decline, paving the way for the Gin Palaces.

In 1825 to 1826, the popularity of gin was rising again, but rather than investing in the Dram Shop, the Gin Palace was created, taking gin to a more upmarket clientele. They were glamours buildings with large glass windows, gas lights, high ceilings, ornate mirrors and comfortable seating that meant patrons could sit and enjoy their gin in a grand atmosphere. These Gin Palaces influenced some of the more ornate Public Houses as well. Though none of the original Gin Palaces remain, three places in London have a similar style of those original Gin Palaces. These are the Viaduct Tavern, the Princess Louise Pub and the Punch Tavern.

The Victorian Era was when the labels of class first came into common usage. These were the working class, the middle class and the upper class. The Working Class were unskilled and skilled labourers who worked in fields, mines of factories as workers. The Middle Class were those who owned businesses in commerce, industry or practised some form of profession such as doctor, solicitor, clergy, teacher, and governess.

The Upper Class were those who were part of the hereditary aristocracy and those who were extremely successful in business, generating a lot of wealth that moved them from the Middle Class to the Upper Class.

From previous historical notes, you may know that I am a big fan of Elizabeth Fry and all that she did during her life to improve the lives and rights of children, women and men. Known for her work to end Child Labour and reforming prisons, she was also one of the key people in the history of modern nursing. She established the first nursing school and even influence her distant relative - the one and only Florence Nightingale - leading her to nursing and all the discoveries she made. Elizabeth Fry also worked for better housing for the poor, the establishment of soup kitchens, education for working women and a reform of the convict prison ship system. Without Elizabeth Fry, the world we live in now would be very different and all the poorer for it.

Victorian Breakfast for the upper class often included porridge, eggs, bacon and fish - the beginnings of what would become known as the Full English Breakfast.

Beds in the Victorian Age were something quite extraordinary. They were the central focus of the bedroom. The frames were made from cast-iron or brass and could be covered with canopies, drapes, pillows, ribbons as well as sheets, spreads and blankets. Mattresses became more developed and better than sacks of straw on the floor for most, though the very poor could still be found sleeping on them.

Doctors notes and early charts have been found that existed back at the start of the 19th century. However, they were not like the clinical medical records that we would know today. I took some liberties with the idea of charts, but there would be some records for payments that were kept by hospitals as the NHS was not established until 1948.

Charles Dickens *The Pickwick Papers* was the first novel that Dickens published. It was serialised in March 1836 and published as a novel in 1837, becoming something of a publishing phenomenon with pirated copies and even theatrical performances of the story. I was originally going to use *The Tenant of Wildfell Hall*, by Anne Brontë, but it wasn't published until 1848, almost a decade after this story is set. I highly recommend both books.

The Victorian Age was still an age of great explorers and adventurers. Explorers had a high standing in Victorian Society and were well-respected. They were the original celebrities, though they often had little care for their fame and were only interested in their next great adventure. Notable Victorian Explorers include Richard Burton, John Hanning Speke, James Augustus Grant, Samuel Baker, Florence von Sass, Henry Morton Stanley and David Livingstone.

Governesses in Victorian England were women from good middle class families that had no money. Raised to be ladies, they couldn't go out and work beside working class girls in ships, but instead could teach at girls' schools or become a governess in the home of an upper class family who needed someone to teach their daughters. A governess in an upper class home not only brought a level of prestige to the household but also told everyone that the lady of that house was too genteel to teach her own children. She had servants to clean her house and a servant to teach her children, raising her status to new heights.

Lancashire Hotpot is a dish that dates back to 1750. It began as a stew that would be cooked in the oven rather than a stew that was cooked over an open flame. The top of the stew was covered with suet dumplings and is often served with pickled red cabbage. When you have a good Lancashire Hotpot, you'll discover that it is an excellent winter dish and a delicious way of filling your belly.

Whisky and brandy are known as warming spirits. They can be taken medicinally, for colds and a number of other ailments. You may be aware of the flasks of brandy that St. Bernards carried around their neck when looking for those lost on snowy mountainsides, but there is one story about the power of these warming spirits that I find to illustrate how effective they can be, and that is the story Colin Maud and his one hour stint in the Arctic Ocean. Colin Douglas "Mad" Maud was a British Navy Officer, who in 1942, took over the captaincy of the destroyer, *Somali* when the captain was taken ill. The *Somali* was torpedoed, and whilst being towed to safety, she sank. Maud was in the freezing Arctic Ocean for an hour.

After Maud went into the water, he drank a bottle of whisky to keep himself warm, something that he credited his survival to. After that, he ordered every man under his command to carry a bottle of whisky should they fall into a similar situation. It was unsurprisingly a very popular order. Colin Maud was Beach Master of Juno Beach during the Normandy Landings (in the movie *The Longest Day*, he's the character with the dog on the beach).

Depression is something that I have briefly touched upon in this story with Mr Hunter's reaction to the loss of his child and Lady Sarah sick in hospital. Depression can strike anyone at any time and how it manifests will be different from person to person. When suffering from depression, it is not a simple thing to pull yourself together and carry on with life. It can be a debilitating thing that can destroy your motivation to do anything as well as your relationships with your family and friends. If you are suffering from depression, then there is no need to suffer alone and try to struggle through it on your own. Help is available around the world. Below are numbers for those who are depressed and need to speak with an experienced counsellor. These are just a few options, there are more you can reach out to.

UK - Samaritans (24 hours) - 116 123

New Zealand - Lifeline Aotearoa Incorporated (24 hours) - 0800 543 354

USA - Substance Abuse and Mental Health Services Administration (SAMHSA) - 1-800-662-4357

Canada - Hope for Wellness Help Line - 1-855-242-3310

Australia - beyondblue (24 hours) - 1300 22 4636

Please do not suffer in silence.

About the Author

I was born in Macclesfield, Cheshire, UK, and raised in the nearby town of Wilmslow. From an early age I discovered I had a flair and passion for writing.

I began writing at the age of 7 and was first published in 2010. I currently live with my partner, Matt, and our two cats in Christchurch, New Zealand.

As an avid horsewoman and gamer, I also have a passion for singing, dancing, the theatre, and my garden.

Facebook: https://www.facebook.com/AuthorC.S.Woolley

Instagram: https://www.instagram.com/thecswoolley

Website: http://mightierthanthesworduk.com

Acknowledgements

Writing can be an extremely lonely profession at times, but thankfully I never have to go through any of the pressures alone. My wonderful Matthew has been a source of constant support to me during all of my writing endeavours since we first met. I couldn't ask for a more fitting partner to share my life or love with.

Writing is not something I stumbled into either, my mother, Helen, took me, and my sisters, to the library every weekend when we were young to get different books, and I always maxed out the number of books I could get. Not only did she encourage me to read, but to write as well. To say I have been writing stories and poetry since I was 7 is not an exaggeration and the development of my writing career is due in no small part to her.

My mother-in-law, Lesley, has also been a source of unflinching and unwavering support, something I could not do without.

To Laura and Sam, who have read and offered opinions, death threats and encouragement on my early drafts, you are true treasures. Amy, you too are worth your weight and more in gold for all your love and support.

It may seem that writers only function alone, but I am blessed to be part of an amazing community of authors whom I know that I have helped push me to even greater heights and success. So to Quinn Ward, Donna Higton, Scarlett Braden Moss, Bryan Cohen, Chez Churton, Robert Scanlon, Jen Lassalle, Brittany Weese, Phoebe Ravencroft, and Marcel Liemant, my dear friends, thank you.

And finally, to you, dear reader, without you there would be no books, no series, no career. I want to thank you for all the time that you spend reading my work, reviewing it, sharing it with your friends and family. Without you there would be nothing. Thank you from the bottom of my heart.

Until we meet again in my next book, thank you and adieu.